They wrested her from her native Hawaii and shut her up in a gloom-filled, chilly mansion on the mainland. There, she spent the next thirteen of her growing-up years.

And as she grew, so grew the threats, the loneliness, the terror. But still, she had not forgotten the lessons of love and brotherhood practiced in Hawaii, which she had learned at the knee of her mother, who was now dead.

And now she was back in Hawaii to claim her inheritance. The inheritance was far richer than she could have imagined—but with it went danger and intrigue. . . .

This book is admiringly dedicated to Mark Egan, Managing Director, North America, Hawaiian Visitors Bureau. His concept of brotherhood and gracious living epitomizes the true aloha spirit of all Hawaii. May that spirit of our fiftieth and newest State pervade all the other forty-nine!

Thunder Over The Reefs

PAULA MINTON

PRESTIGE BOOKS · NEW YORK

THUNDER OVER THE REEFS

PRESTIGE BOOKS INC. • 18 EAST 41ST STREET
NEW YORK, N.Y. 10017

Chapter
ONE

PHILLIP MASON stood on the porch of his house, which overlooked the magnificent beach of Waimanalo, and uttered a sigh of deep content. Beyond the shimmering white sandy crescent beach stretched the endless blue of the Pacific, and yet it was not the same unending blue. It was no wonder that the Hawaiians had named it Wainani—"beautiful water." One had but to stare at it and watch the blue give way to tones of green as bright as the ti plant and as dull and ominous as the leaves of the jade vine or the bipinnate leaves of the jacaranda. Again, when storms were brewing, there would be a murky blue that was almost black beneath the surface of the waters, and to his right, where Makapuu Point stretched its obdurate fingers into the ocean, one could almost imagine that the blackness heralded the dangerous reefs. The ocean was like a woman, variable in moods, the water dappled with the sun running across it and touching it as with a lover's caress; or it would lie silent and brooding, when the sky was dull, as if waiting for the brightness of a new day to illumine its endless surface. And there were tones of purple that mixed with azure, but over all the greens and the blues as endless in variety as the shades set forth in a dress designer's book.

It was an island, and yet it was a paradise. It was a refuge, and yet it was home. It was all beauty, and all truth, to Philip Mason after his years of struggle and illness.

It was the renewal of a life he had once thought not worth living, and it was the fulfillment of a promise whose dream he had doubted. It was the island of Oahu, the third largest of the Hawaiian Islands. He smiled comfortably as the thought came to him, from his days in Chicago as a schoolteacher, that he had often lectured on this territory to the students in his geography class at Butler High School. He had only to close his eyes to visualize himself back in that dusty classroom, hearing the drone of his own voice, sensing the indifference and restlessness of the pupils who hoped that the bell would rescue them from this last class of the day and send them out shouting and jostling to the recreation ground, to the soda fountain, to their adolescent prancing about the girls who took their fancy.

There had been a map tacked up on the blackboard, he remembered, and he had stood there tracing the extent of this vast virgin territory with the tip of his pointer. And he had said that Hawaii stretched from Kure Island, fifteen hundred miles northwest of Honolulu, to its southernmost point, which was an isolated oceanographic station known as South Point at the southern tip of the main island of Hawaii. He had told them that Kure was just one and a half miles long by half a mile wide and comprised mainly sand, coral, and scrub brush. And now the map and the pointer were gone, and in their place there was this house and this beach and his beloved wife, Milliama, and their first child, whom he had christened Audrey in memory of his own shy, lovely sister who had died of rheumatic fever at the age of fourteen. And because Milliama had been born on Oahu of parents who themselves had come to Hawaii from Polynesia long years ago, he had learned the Hawaiian language, and in Milliama's presence he called his tiny daughter Aukele, which is the Hawaiian for Audrey.

It was evening; yet the sun still smiled upon the blue water that stretched to the end of the horizon and beyond his vision. Gentle waves rolled in upon the glistening white sands almost five hundred yards away from the house his Hawaiian neighbors had helped him build. Indeed, he had done very little, because he had been a schoolteacher and an ailing one at that, but his neighbors had been staunch friends, and they had laughed and sung and made a festival of building this strange and beautiful house for the *haole*—the white man— who had come to live among them. And when the house was finished, they had held a great *luau*, a feast with taro and poi, and pig covered with ti leaves and stuffed with hot lava rocks, then placed in a huge underground oven that they called an *imu*. And then they had toasted him and his bride, Milliama, in *okoleaha*. Philip Mason chuckled at the recollection. With all his pedantic knowledge of the islands during his days as a teacher back in Chicago, he certainly hadn't known that *okoleaha* was Hawaii's only authentic alcoholic beverage. Because, of course, it was part of the image of the schoolteacher that one never drank or smoked. Yet here, thousands of miles away, a lifetime away from Chicago, things were uncomplicated and natural. But best of all, it was the *aloha* of the islands that enchanted him . . . the pervading spirit of friendliness and helpfulness, the lesson of living together in brotherhood that accepted a man for what he was and not for the symbols of his possessions or his place in the social sphere of things. Here there were friends of Japanese, Chinese, Filipino, and intermixed Polynesian extraction. He had never been conscious of their skins or the oddity of their names or speech. And now, with the storm clouds hovering over Europe, with the rumble of guns in Poland and Czechoslovakia and Holland and the ominous goose-stepping cadence of the jackboots of Hitler's armies, this lesson of brotherhood was all the more priceless. Here in this paradise, these islands which had risen from the ancient volcanoes at the bottom of the ocean, the thought of war was a barbaric anachronism. . . .

There was a new life here, and Philip Mason looked forward to it with a joyous eagerness that he had never before known. Of course, he had Milliama to thank for so much of that, as well as, in lesser personal degree, his good friends and neighbors who had helped him build the first house he had ever owned. Now, after five years on Oahu, he could almost identify himself with the life of Hawaii, its fabulous legends and its complex history, its assimilation of Polynesian, Japanese, Chinese, Filipino, and *haole* cultures. For his ties with the mainland were gone, except for his cousin Dan, the son of his father's younger brother. He had gone back just last spring to visit Dan and the latter's wife, Margery, and their two little children, Grover and Beatrice. Grover was two now, and Beatrice was the same age as his own Aukele, just one. He turned back to look into the living room, where black-haired Milliama in a flowery *muu-muu* sat cuddling their baby, her sweetly guileless face beatified by the tender look she bestowed upon the little girl. Aukele was such a good baby, so quiet and gentle, like his own Milliama, he thought. God had been very good to him, to bring him to this new Eden where men could learn the lesson of Christ and Gandhi and others who died to save all men from bigotry and prejudice and hatred.

He caught Milliama's eye and blew a kiss to her, and she blew one back, lowering her eyes with that exquisite modesty which was so characteristic of her and which had so won his heart. Back on the mainland, back in Chicago, there would have been those who would have jeered at him for marrying a Polynesian girl who was brown-skinned and whose English was quaint and interspersed with the Hawaiian idiom, into which she lapsed at the slightest provocation, despite all his good-natured scolding. Here, to love her was as natural as breathing. Now he had all his roots in this ocean-bound territory which dreamed of statehood one day. He would never go back to the mainland, because he belonged here, and he was still a teacher. At McKinley High School, where there were so many *nisei* and all the other races that had come to Hawaii and been drawn into its legendary culture and crafts and arts. The children of Ameri-

8

cans or English or German or Dutch settlers who had married Japanese wives, or again the offspring of Japanese fathers whose wives had been Hawaiian with the Polynesian admixture of centuries past. They were bright, industrious, eager for knowledge, proud of their own racial heritage and yet seeking to be good Americans. They were like his friend James Sakato, who was only nineteen and a *nisei*, and now a soldier in the United States Army and stationed at Schofield Barracks. James had been his brightest pupil, and he might have gone on to become a clerk in an insurance office because he was exceptionally good at mathematics. But he had felt a burning patriotism and had enlisted almost immediately after his graduation. His father, Toguru, had his own little farm over at Ewa, but already Toguru had come to understand the democracy of America. His son had brought home lessons from school and shown the old man that the *haole* ways had merit to them. Yes, here in Hawaii, Philip Mason felt that he had been given a second chance, and he could see the results of his teaching in the warm friendships he had made.

He lit a cigarette and stared out again at the gently breaking waves that came to rest at last over the white sands of the beach. It was a view of which he never tired. In Chicago, there had been Lake Michigan to swim in, but even the scenic view from the Promontory at 55th Street in no way matched the splendor and the color of what he saw here daily. And so there was no reason to feel homesickness for Chicago, though he had grown up as a boy and a young man there, though he had taught school there. His own lineage had come from across the other ocean, for his father, Edward Mason, had been a London printer who initially settled in Boston and then moved to Chicago to work for a thriving letterpress firm. Edward Mason had married a pleasant, unassuming girl who worked as a bookkeeper for that firm, and Philip and Audrey had been their only children. Philip's parents had died while he was still in college, both of them within a week of each other as the result of an influenza

9

epidemic that had claimed many victims from the North Side, where they had lived.

His father had been frugal, but the family had never had very much ready money. Hence, it had been a surprise to Philip Mason to learn that he was the sole heir to a $40,000 insurance policy the payments on which his father had somehow managed to meet in spite of a decade of minor illnesses and many bills. He had banked the money, taken only what he needed to finish his college studies, and then become a teacher, first in a grammar school on the West Side, then in a high school, where, when he was thirty-three, his doctor had told him that he needed a temperate climate, plenty of rest, and wholesome food. "Florida, if you can afford it," the doctor had quipped.

The tests had shown a hint of tuberculosis, so Philip Mason had resigned his job and gone to San Francisco to visit his cousin Dan, who was just getting himself engaged to an attractive if sharp-featured society girl named Margery Gore. Dan had taken over an import shop on O'Farrell Street from his father, Matt Mason, who had been Philip's father's younger brother, had gone to work in the same Chicago letterpress firm for three years, then married and moved to San Francisco, where his own business acumen had led him to invest some of his printer's wages as part owner of a tiny import shop owned by a genial little Chinese. Later he had bought the Chinese out and made the business prosper, so that his son Dan garnered a profitable inheritance after his death.

Dan Mason had expressed concern over his cousin's illness and suggested that Philip take a vacation in Hawaii. So Philip had drawn out money for a round-trip passage on the Matson steamships, which made the trip to Honolulu every twelve days, and funds enough to stay in Honolulu for a month. That had been in the spring of 1936, and the month had lasted more than five years. Philip would be thirty-eight years old tomorrow, but he felt that his life was just beginning on this Saturday, December 6, 1941.

10

Chapter
TWO

JIMMY SAKATO had asked him to come to town this evening and talk to some of Jimmy's friends who wanted to know more about what was going on in Europe. He had tried, in his classes at McKinley, to point out the parallels that history showed down through the ages and the ultimate defeat of the barbarian aggressor. This mad paperhanger who had come into control of a poverty-stricken Germany and imposed a warlike credo on the gullible minds of his people was not far removed from an Attila or a Vercingetorix or a Genghis Khan. In essence, those who sought to conquer by force would die by the sword, as the Bible prophesied. And yet the blood of innocents would be spilled until the insanity was over. Jimmy and his friends feared that Japan would side with Germany and go to war against their own new country of America. He understood what this would mean if war came between Japan and the United States. The young *nisei*, American citizens and proud of their patriotism, would know the horror of fighting on the side of those who would make war against their fathers and their relatives, still loyal to the Emperor. And the old *nisei*, the Japanese immigrants who could not be citizens but who lived in Hawaii, were bound by traditions stronger than their own wills to uphold the destiny of the Empire of the Rising Sun if war should come. There would be many families in Hawaii torn apart and made enemies in two warring camps within the same household. Such was always the tragedy of war, Philip Mason thought sadly.

As for himself, he had no geopolitical beliefs other than an ingenuous and optimistic faith in the ultimate destiny of mankind. In his five years on the islands, he had seen how men could live like brothers, and Hitler's war against the British Empire seemed so far away, so nightmarish. It would be easy to think only of the beauty of his house and his family and the sparkling white beach beyond him and to gaze from the windows of his cupola out across the Pacific and forget that there could be such a thing as war. Yet he was not such a dreamer that he did not realize the imminence of disaster.

Some of the boys in his history class had asked him how it was possible for Germany, its Junkerism crushed into total defeat in the World War, to emerge once again, after only a generation, as a warrior nation that sought "Germany today, tomorrow the world." And he had answered as best he could, saying that there will always be opportunists who seek to aggrandize themselves by playing on the latent hatreds and fears that men hide in their hearts, by turning brother against brother and race against race. He had told them of the burning of the books and the isolation of the Jews into ghettoes and the infamous yellow Star of David armbands that every Jew must wear in Germany so that he could be singled out for persecution. He chuckled as he remembered the quaint remark of Tommy Ching, a bright-eyed fifteen-year-old son of a Chinese dockworker, who was capable of writing commendable quatrains in English as good as he himself used. Tommy had shaken his head, raised his hand, and piped up, "Maybe it's only the *haoles* who are crazy, Mr. Mason. Maybe they ought to come to Oahu and see how everybody gets along with everybody else."

Yes, that was a lesson he himself had learned by coming to the islands.

It had been Milliama's own father who had sold him the acre of land on which this house of theirs had been built. His name was Kalaiki, and he had come to Oahu forty years ago from the Polynesian island of Raiatea, where he had been a headman of his tribe. Kalaiki had been a gifted fisherman, and one day he had discovered a bed of flawless seed pearls in a narrow lagoon, guarded by a giant squid, which he had killed with his knife. When a plague broke out in Raiatea, he had taken his pearls and come to Oahu. Having sold the pearls in Honolulu to a Chinese jeweler who had given him a fair price, Kalaiki had banked the money and soon after bought twenty acres of land near Waimanalo, including that section on which Philip Mason's house now stood. Ten years after he had acquired this land, Kalaiki had married a buxom young Hawaiian girl, Malia, whose own parents had come from Papeete. They had had only one child, the lovely Milliama, and Malia had died of a fever three years after the birth of her daughter. Not long after that, Kalaiki had married and had two sons and a daughter by his second wife, Llani, who had taken care of Milliama as if the girl had been her very own. Kalaiki had seen to it that some of the money from the sale of the pearls had been spent to give Milliama a good education, and he had even engaged a *haole* teacher for the girl to supplement what she learned in the village grammar school. Then he had enrolled her at McKinley, and that was where Philip had met her, as one of his own students.

Philip Mason lit another cigarette and looked out at the odd rock formation of the tiny island to his left, shaped like a crouching rabbit and hence so named. Yes, he had thought of staying only a month or so in Oahu; but the friendliness of the people, the mild climate, and the breathtaking beauty of the land and the ocean had cast an infrangible spell upon him.

The month had stretched into a year, and then when he had felt that his health was better, he had wanted to take an active part in forming young minds, just as he had back in Chicago. Fortunately, there had been an opening as a substitute teacher at McKinley High School, and by the end of his second year, he had been offered a regular teacher's post. Milliama had entered his class that year, he remembered, just sixteen and a sophomore, reticent and shy, seldom volunteering to recite. Yet he had been struck by the probing keenness of her mind, revealed by her written themes and the oral and written examinations he gave.

Her father had come to visit him one evening at the little boardinghouse on Lewers where he had stayed ever since his arrival in Honolulu. Kalaiki spoke English well, and was a man of simple dignity. It was easy to understand that he had been a chief back in Raiatea. And he had thanked Philip Mason with a grave and exquisite courtesy for having given Milliama such enthusiasm for her work, such an avid interest in reading the *haole* books. That meeting had led to a lasting friendship. And later, when Kalaiki had asked Philip Mason if he would not like to have his own house and to live within sight of the ocean and he had eagerly agreed, Kalaiki told him that he would sell him an acre of land, the loveliest of all on Waimanalo, for only five hundred American dollars.

Overjoyed, Philip Mason had bought the land and had the deed recorded. He had put the official document in an oilskin pouch and stuffed it into a giant conch shell, which he had found one March afternoon on the leeward side, near Waianae. It had been half-buried in the sand, and he had stumbled across it, lifted it, shaken out the sand, and put it to his ear. And it had seemed to him that he could hear the eerie music of the ocean rising from the bottomless depths and held captive within the conch, and it had become his favorite symbol of the islands.

Kalaiki and other friends whom he had made after that first meeting with Milliama's kindly father had advised him how to build the house—and then had overwhelmed him by building it themselves. A Matson steamer brought from San Francisco the cargo of strong, moisture-resistant redwood to form the sidings of the two-story house, whose foundation was built upon volcanic rock. That in itself was still another symbol, since all Hawaii had been born eons ago from the volcanic craters beneath the blue Pacific that, century upon century, sent their sediment up to the surface till at last land was formed.

Building the house to the specifications he had always longed for had taken more than half his inheritance, but it had been money well spent. Five stairs of black volcanic rock rose to the spacious veranda. The rails at each side of the steps, as well as those along the veranda, were made of gleaming koa wood, on which Milliama's father had carved in ornate scrolls the Hawaiian words that would conjure up the good spirits and bless the house of his *haole* friend and the teacher of his daughter. On one rail there was the word *malulani*, which meant "under heaven's protection"; on the other, there were the words *kealoha* and *uwao*, which meant "the loved one" and "the peacemaker." The cupola, topped by a spired weathervane, housed a kind of attic room above the second floor ascended to by a winding stairway, and it was here that Philip Mason loved to sit in his wicker chair and gaze out upon the Pacific in its varying moods. There was a huge chimney in the center of the roof, its flues connecting with the great rock fireplace between the living and dining rooms and with the primitive stone kitchen oven. Kalaiki, a skilled woodworker, had carved a mantlepiece made of *oahi* wood for the fireplace, and on this lustrous wood he had engraved a picture story that showed how Philip Mason, "he who works with books," had come across the sea to teach the children of Hawaii the lessons of love and peace.

There were sharp eaves and gables, with casement windows on the second floor. It resembled a Gothic house Philip had seen illustrated when he was a boy. His father had shown him the picture in a book, and Philip had never forgotten it.

And then there had been the great *luau* to dedicate and bless the house. And Milliama had danced before him as he sat with her father passing the coconut shell of *oko-leaha* back and forth around the circle of celebrants. She

15

had placed a red hibiscus over her right ear, and she had smiled at him, and he had trembled with his awareness of her young, supple, brown-skinned beauty. And then her father had whispered to him, with a chuckle, "You have not learned all the traditions of our islands, revered teacher of my daughter, or you would know that Milliama dances for you and that when a maiden wears the flower of passion over her right ear, it is a sign that she has not yet chosen a man."

And that was how it had happened. Six months later, after Milliama's graduation from high school, he had married her in the little Episcopalian church near Bishop's Museum, and then, in the beautiful garden that her father and her father's friends had helped him plant, there had been a Hawaiian ceremony to make the wedding doubly meaningful. Now their child had blessed their union. God had been very good to him indeed.

Not every islander owned land in this paradise of the Pacific. He no longer felt like a *haole,* but rather as one of the people who had come from distant lands to share the simplicity and the dignity of this good life with all its meaningful inspiration to all men of good faith who were not blinded by hatred and greed and lust for power. And he had shown Milliama the deed to their land, telling her that this was the token of their belonging to each other upon this soil, and that one day Aukele would inherit it and live in happiness as they would live now. And he had buried the conch shell with the oilskin pouch inside it under the shade of a giant papaya tree that Kalaiki had himself planted when ground had been broken for the construction of the house.

Milliama had put Aukele back into her crib and was preparing the simple evening meal of *Mahimahi,* the bland-tasting dolphin fish, fresh papaya, and *haupia,* a delicious pudding made of arrowroot, coconut, and pineapple served on a ti leaf. "You won't mind too much, Milliama, if I stay overnight in Honolulu with the boys?" Philip Mason anxiously asked his beautiful young wife.

"No, my husband, why should I mind anything that

16

gives you pleasure?" Milliama replied in her soft, melodious voice. "Only do not forget that tomorrow is your birthday and that my father and his friends will prepare a true *ahaaina* in your honor."

Philip Mason reached for his wife's slim hand and drew it to his lips. "Your father is too good to me, my darling one," he murmured. "He gave me this land, and then he gave you to me, and I did not begin to live until I met you. And now he reminds me of the ancient Hawaiian customs, for the *ahaaina* is the word that means the gathering of friends to eat, and it came long before the *luau,* isn't that right, Milliama?"

She nodded, her long lashes veiling those marvelous dark eyes, always exquisitely shy, a quality at which he had never ceased to marvel. "My father says that you have the spirit of the islands in you and that you do not seem to be like the *haole* who came to take instead of to give," she whispered.

He put his hands gently on her shoulders and bent to kiss her forehead. "I respect your father as a chief, Milliama. I have learned much from his wisdom."

For a moment she looked up at him, her eyes grave and wistful. "Are you never homesick for the mainland, my husband?"

He shook his head. "My life is here with you and Aukele and with my pupils, darling one. Where else on the mainland is there so much beauty as on this island?" Then he put his lips to her ear and added in an adoring whisper, "Or as in this house, my beloved?"

He left the house and walked down toward the beach for a last look at the ocean before he drove the jeep to town. It was a second-hand jeep, but Philip Mason was as proud of it as many a millionaire would have been of a Mercedes-Benz. Mostly, he was proud of the new skill he had in learning to drive, for in Chicago he had once vowed that he would never get behind the wheel of an automobile. Surely, Hawaii had been rebirth for him in so many ways.

The sun was setting, and now the myriad blues of the

ocean imitated the riotous palette of a master artist . . . there were piercing indigo and pale china and then another blue that was nearly green, and there was the soft, muted pastel blue of dusk over the calm surface of the waters. At the edge of the beach, the tiny waves broke gently and crawled lazily upon the white sands. There was peace and stillness and warmth to the air. Philip Mason drew in a deep breath and closed his eyes, and indelibly the vision he had just seen was repeated for him. *Let it be always thus,* he said to himself.

Even in his khaki uniform of a private in the United States Army, Jimmy Sakato was still the same tall, slim, poised youth who had been such a revelation in his class. Jimmy—he hated the name James—was as strongly Americanized as any of his students back in Chicago, Philip Mason felt. He was impatient with the archaic and with traditions that had no practical usage. He had argued and cajoled and reasoned with his parents that today was the way of American democracy, not that of the samurai and the Emperor, that Hawaii was a land of promise linked with the mainland and its limitless future.

He and four other boys from McKinley High who had joined the army and who, like himself, had once been Philip Mason's students, had had tea and rice cakes with their teacher in a tiny Japanese restaurant on South King Street, and then Philip Mason had offered to stand them all treat at the historic old "House without a Key" of the Halekulani. This beautiful garden-inn offered its gracious homelike hospitality to the tourists who were beginning to discover the wonders of Waikiki Beach. Farther down along the beach stood the pink stucco palace of the Royal Hawaiian and the other Matson-owned hotel, the Moana. In the dark sky, the twinkling light of a plane en route to Hilo on the big island winked its pathway, competing with the bright stars. Their smiling little waiter had brought them huge glasses of iced tea atop which orchids floated and in which thick sticks of fresh pineapple rose above the brim. In the adjacent Hau Terrace, a late cocktail party for newly arrived guests was going on, and there was the sound of music and the tinkle of glasses and the murmur of voices.

"I'm worried, Mr. Mason," Jimmy Sakato confided. "There's lots of talk about war now. If it comes, the old-timers will suffer. And the trouble is, even though they're Japanese to the core and preserve the old traditions, they've never been back to Japan and they've lived all their lives here. Yet they'll be treated like enemies, I'm afraid. I've been preaching that to my father and mother for a long time now, and they've got good sense. But I don't know about the other families."

"The tragedy is, Jimmy, that war solves nothing and makes bitter enemies of those who have long been friends," Philip Mason sadly replied. He knew this was no answer, and yet it was the only one he had. Always an idealist, even when he had begun as a teacher in his mid-twenties back in a little Chicago grammar school, he had tried to gloss over the lurid accounts of wars in the history books, minimizing their importance. But Hitler's war wasn't something you could banish just by sticking your head in the sand and pretending it didn't exist, and the militaristic powers of Japan were being forced with their backs against an economic wall. War was inevitable, and yet it would be tragic and horrifying, as it had been from the beginning of time.

"There's scuttlebutt at the barracks that we may go to Europe and maybe even the Mediterranean," Jimmy Sakato continued, twirling the swizzle stick in his glass of iced tea.

Henry Katanabe, the son of a sugar-cane worker who had moved from Hilo a decade ago, had joined the army right after his graduation from McKinley. He reached over for the orchid in Jimmy's glass and held it up. "You should worry, Jimmy," he joked. "Take along lots of these when you meet those cute European *wahines*. You'll be a great success!" And everybody laughed as the tension was eased for the moment.

19

Because Jimmy was on weekend liberty, he urged Philip Mason to come with them to a little Japanese theater where a Noh play was being produced. And it was well after midnight when they emerged out into the darkened street and headed for the YMCA. Philip Mason had promised his star pupils to have breakfast with them and then drive them out to the Pali, from whose majestic terrace one could see the verdant lowlands of windward Oahu and over which, according to legend, the warriors of Kamehameha the Great had pushed the soldiers of Kalanikupule to their deaths in the battle of 1795 that established the empire of Hawaii.

The night had been exhilarating, and it had been well past midnight when he finally bunked down in his room at the YMCA along with Jimmy and Pablo Hernandez, a stocky Filipino who had been one of his earliest pupils and was now wearing the two chevrons of a corporal. He felt a little selfish at having left Milliama and the baby so he could "have a night with the boys," but he knew that she would understand. Especially if his best boys were going to be shipped out to fight against the Nazis, Milliama would know that he would want to see them for perhaps the last time. They were as close to him as if they had been his own sons. This was one of the true rewards of his profession, watching the adolescents mature into serious young men who looked to the future and who had ideas of their own on how to shape it. So he didn't fall asleep right away but dozed off till he was suddenly aware of what sounded like thunder. Blinking his eyes and sitting up, he heard it closer, in the direction of Pearl Harbor and Wheeler Field. Jimmy Sakato was already awake and scrambling into his uniform. "Something's wrong over down by Pearl, Mr. Mason," Jimmy said excitedly. "Us guys better get back to Schofield."

"I'll drive you there in the jeep. Let's go," Philip Mason agreed as he hastily dressed. Glancing at his wristwatch, he saw that it was only a few minutes after seven.

He had parked the jeep last night at the curb outside the YMCA. The boys piled in, and he got behind the

20

wheel and drove off toward the barracks. The sounds of thunder grew more frequent; yet the sky was a serene blue. "Look!" Jimmy Sakato pointed straight ahead. Two planes were veering down from the blue sky toward Pearl Harbor, the emblem of the Rising Sun on their left underwings. "Those are Zeros, Japanese planes, they're attacking us!"

Philip Mason stepped on the gas, and the jeep bounced along Waianae Avenue toward the Headquarters Building. As they neared the gates, another Zero dipped from the sky and swept down northward, its noseguns spitting fire. Jimmy Sakato stood up with a gurgling cry, then collapsed over the windshield. As the plane roared overhead, Philip Mason felt a heavy blow strike him between the shoulderblades. His vision blurred. His hands gripped the wheel in a last convulsive tension, and he gasped, "Milliama . . . Aukele . . . I want to—"

The jeep swung crazily with its load of dead and dying and crashed into the stone post beside the gate of Schofield Barracks.

Chapter
THREE

MILLIAMA MASON did not learn of her husband's death until late that fateful Sunday evening. She, too, had been wakened by the sounds of the bombing of Pearl Harbor, and the child Aukele had wakened also and had started to cry. As she soothed the infant, Milliama's lovely young face was taut with anxiety, knowing that Philip was in Honolulu with his young soldier friends and perhaps in the very area where the bombs were falling.

Turning on the radio, she learned the official news of the Japanese attack, and then there were the long hours of waiting. Yet for the baby's sake, she went about her tasks with a quiet intensity, preparing food for the little girl and feeding her just as she always did, with the same teasing little jokes and happy laughter. Yes, Aukele was too young to understand, but perhaps Philip was all right and would stay in a safe place of shelter until all was over.

It was her father, Kalaiki, who brought her the news just as she was sitting down to supper. His face was grave, and he had tears in his eyes that he did not try to hide as he came into the house and went to her. She caught her breath and rose. Aukele in her high chair gurgled happily at the sight of her grandfather and reached out her spoon toward him, knocking the little dish of baby food onto the floor.

"Father—it is Philip, isn't it?" Milliama said slowly.

"Yes, my daughter. As soon as I heard the news of the

23

planes that attacked the big ships, I went into town to see my friend Ito Toguri. He has the teahouse near the Kawaiakao Church, and his eldest son was a pupil of your husband. The boy is a sailor on the U.S.S. *Arizona*. Ito sent his other two sons out to find out what they could. It is a terrible thing, this war, because Ito and his sons will be thought of as our enemies."

"But you have not told me, Father. I can be brave. Was—was Philip hurt?"

Kalaika bowed his head and closed his eyes. "I have lost a son, Milliama. And poor Ito has lost his also, for the battleship has sunk and those upon it died from the bombs, dropped by the planes from the East. I would to God I did not have to bring you such news, my daughter."

"Do—do you know how he died, Father?"

The old man nodded. "Ito has a good friend who works for the *Advertiser*. He reports the news, and he learned that Philip was killed. His pupils in the jeep with him also, Milliama. The bullets from the gun of a plane that fired upon the soldiers at Schofield killed them all. But it was a quick death, without pain. This you must remember, Milliama. I have lost a dear son, and my grief is as great as yours. We must comfort each other, my daughter."

And then, seeing her father weep, her own grief came upon her, and they clung to each other in their desolation, while the baby banged upon the table with her spoon, not knowing what to make of the sight she beheld but happy that the two whom she knew and loved were close at hand.

"There was not time to say farewell to my husband." Milliama at last dried her tears and spoke with a toneless anguish. "He loved Hawaii so, my father. He will be close to me always."

"We shall give him burial on this land, then."

Milliama shook her head. "No, my father. That would not have been his wish. We were both so much in love we did not think that death would come so soon. But once, early in our marriage, he spoke of his happiness here and his feeling that when he should die, he wished to become a part of the islands that he loved. Not to mark his grave with a stone, as is the custom on the mainland, this I know he did not wish. I will scatter his ashes over the stairway to this our house where his child was born, so that he will be part of it always." She turned back to the table and bent to Aukele, picked the child up in her arms, and kissed her, weeping again.

Kalaika uttered a long sigh. "It shall be as you say, my daughter. He was a good man. One did not think of him as being a stranger or a foreigner. In his heart there was love and faith and hope."

"I wish only that I could have given him a son to carry on his name, O my father," Milliama sobbed. "But I will bring Aukele up to know how gentle and how good her father was so that she too will love the islands as he did. It may be that in her time she will teach others just as Philip did. And there will be peace again, O my father."

And thus it was that the body of Philip Mason, instead of being interred in the Pacific National Memorial Cemetery in Punchbowl Crater, the resting-place of those from the Pacific areas who died in World War II, was cremated and his ashes sprinkled over the stone steps that led to the house where he had known supreme and final happiness with Milliama. . . .

On the same day that Philip Mason died, and only about four hours after the first bombs had fallen on Hickam Field and the battleships and destroyers and docks at Pearl Harbor, Lieutenant General Walter C. Short became military governor of the Territory of Hawaii. From then until October 24, 1944, this island paradise was under martial law. It was a time for drastic social changes, a new order that was destined to lead to statehood, but only after sociological and economic trials that were to bring a new understanding of the need for change and adaptation. The *nisei* who fought valiantly in the 100th Battalion and the famous volunteer 442d Regimental Combat Team indisputably proved the honor of their people in Hawaii and paid their own debt of honor to the country of their birth. When they returned to Hawaii, they could tell their parents and neighbors what they had learned of fears and prejudices in foreign lands where they had fought and where so many of them had died.

For Milliama Mason and her daughter, Aukele, the war was a time of dedication to each other. Milliama, young and beautiful, the owner of a house on lovely Waimanalo Beach and heiress to the money in the Honolulu Bank that remained of Philip Mason's own legacy, was coveted by many an eligible bachelor. Even Kalaiki urged her to remarry so that Aukele might have the guidance of a father. But this Milliama steadfastly refused to do, even though her step-mother, the handsome and gentle Llani, herself tried to induce the young widow to put aside her grief and think seriously of resuming the life to which every normal young woman is destined.

"No, honored mother," Milliama deferentially replied —for in the true tradition of the islands she respected Llani as she had her own mother—"I cannot again love any man as I did Philip. I will bring up his child as he would have wished. She is an American, and she shall have an education and the care given a child on the mainland."

"Your feelings do you credit, my daughter," Llani said with a gracious smile, "but it is wise to be sensible. It is true that there is money in the bank to pay for the child's food and clothing, but it will not last forever, and these are difficult times. You know yourself what the cost of food and clothing is at the stores because we are at war, Milliama. And he would not have wished you to remain without a man the rest of your life. You are still so young."

But Milliama was not swayed by that argument. She rejoiced in the fate that had given her a *haole* education; if she had not gone to McKinley and learned English so well that she could qualify for admission, she might never have met Philip Mason and known the short but rapturously sweet years of their union. Aukele had been the fruit of their love, and she would devote her life to her daughter. As for the money, when the war began, there was about $10,000 left of Philip's father's insurance. She proposed to spend all of it for Aukele; she herself needed little, and she could work to supplement this capital. She was an excellent seamstress and could make her own clothing as well as the child's. And dear Philip had told her that the taxes must be paid every year so that this house and this glorious stretch of beach could never be taken away from them. The money in the bank would make sure of that.

Philip Mason had become an excellent swimmer, and during his courting of Milliama, the two of them had spent many an idyllic hour together swimming in Waimanalo Bay or off the beach at Waikiki. Milliama's father, despite his mature age, had been a gifted swimmer and surfer almost from his very boyhood, and he had taught Milliama how to enjoy the exhilarating sport of riding the waves, both with board and with one's own body. In turn, Milliama had shown Philip how to use the surfboard and to ride the crest of the gentle waves along Waikiki Beach. And so, when Aukele was eighteen months old, Milliama took her down to the shores of their sandy beach and initiated her baby daughter in paddling and wading so that she would have no fear of the blue waters of the Pacific and would in time be as expert as her mother and her grandfather. These magical hours, spent together on the white sand and the placid and shallow water just offshore under the brilliant blue sky, were an anodyne for Milliama's grief.

Aukele was a happy child, always laughing, always eager to play. And it seemed to Milliama that the spirit of Philip Mason was with them. For had he not become part of this earth and sky and water through the symbol of her having strewn his ashes over the steps leading to their house? There were times, toward twilight, when the magnificent orange ball of the sun dwindled in its cradle of riotous colors before giving way to the soft stillness of night, when Milliama felt the ache of longing for her man, and then she would close her eyes and pretend that he was there on the beach beside her, and it was almost as if she could hear his voice and, as the soft trade wind caressed her hair and shoulders, as if he were caressing her once again.

But the money in the bank did not last quite so long as Milliama had expected. For one thing, two years after Philip Mason's death, Milliama's father was taken violently ill one evening while having supper with his daughter and adored little granddaughter. The major surgery that followed this seizure was costly, as was Kalaiki's slow convalescence, and Milliama saw to it that he had the very best of care. Since his own meager income had been stopped because of his long illness, Milliama paid the taxes on his house and land. She devoted several afternoons a week to volunteer work for the Red Cross and the USO, while Llani and occasionally Llani's daughter Luka cared for Aukele. But by the time her father had recovered and was able to walk about with the aid of a cane, Milliama had decided that it was time to find gainful employment. There were not many clerical jobs for civilians, and the wages would be as paltry, as those for seamstress work. She was practical enough to realize that her physical attractiveness and her skill as a dancer could earn a great deal more, especially at a time when soldiers and sailors, as well as the civilian population able to afford it, sought distraction from the war.

So Milliama found work in a small pseudo-Polynesian cabaret on Kalakaua Avenue that was owned by an enterprising pair of Chinese brothers. To a noisily appreciative audience of servicemen, with a spotlight playing upon her sinuous, graceful body, Milliama performed traditional Tahitian dances and the sensationally Westernized hula, sometimes varying her entertainment by singing old island songs while she accompanied herself on the ukelele. Many a handsome young *haole* sailor or soldier was eager to date her after the show, but not once did she accept. She begrudged the hours away from little

28

Aukele, though it was a relief to watch the diminished bank balance grow and to know that the money would safeguard Aukele's future.

Civilians could not journey from the mainland to Hawaii during the war, but Philip's cousin Dan wrote to Milliama several times a month. He intimated that he and his wife would be happy to take Aukele and rear her as their own child if ever Milliama wished. She wrote back, using the formal language that her dead husband had found so charmingly quaint when she had been his pupil, that she was grateful for their concern but that she wished Aukele to grow up on the island and to know the fulfillment of her life here, where there was always beauty to inspire the eye and the heart. Dan Mason read those letters aloud to his wife, Margery, and both of them laughed at the young woman's lofty phrases, but with a sense of relief. For Dan Mason had made the offer to Milliama out of a sense of family obligation to his dead cousin. He did not actually wish to add another member to his household. The war had had its effects on the mainland, too, and his shop was hardly making profit enough to care for his own family.

"One thing about it, honey," he told Margery after reading one of these letters. "Philip's wife is probably pretty well off. She owns the house and the land it's on outright. Maybe when the war's over and the tourists start flowing back to Honolulu, she and her kid will be a lot better off than we are."

Those words were spoken with a kind of cynical envy. Margery Mason smiled and nodded, and then the matter was forgotten. But the underlying concept behind Dan Mason's envying comment was to have a greater bearing on the lives of Dan and Margery Mason than either of them could ever have guessed. For Audrey Mason, whose mother still thought of her as Aukele, a child born of love and meant to live on this island paradise where she herself had found such happiness, it was to have the most profound meaning of all.

Chapter
FOUR

It was the summer of 1947, the year after the disastrous seventy-nine-day strike of all plantation workers in the sugar industry. That strike had been one of the tremendous sociological changes taking place in Hawaii after the end of the war. And there were other changes in store for the islands. Now everyone was talking about the bill that Joseph Farrington, delegate to Congress from the Territory of Hawaii, had succeeded in conveying through the House of Representatives to approve statehood for Hawaii by a vote of 196 to 133. To the *kamaaina*—the old-time residents of the islands—this transition from monarchy to United States territory to what seemed imminent statehood was incredible.

Old Kalaiki, who in his youth had himself been a chief under a monarchy, enthusiastically told his friends that great advantages could accrue to the islands if the Senate were to confirm the action of the House of Representatives. But it was not to be that year, nor was Milliama's father destined to realize his hope. In September he fell ill of the recurrent complaint that had originally hospitalized him and died a few days after having been stricken.

At the little cemetery near Punaluu, Milliama wept bitterly as she saw her father's coffin being lowered into the earth. This outward show of bereavement, which she had not shown at the time of Philip's death, was in reality her pent-up grief for the loss of her beloved husband. Her father's passing had reminded her all too poignantly of how he had revealed to Philip the secret of her love for him. And now the two persons dearest to her in all the world had gone, and she clutched Aukele to her in an anguish of fear, lest the little girl be taken from her too. Her half-brothers, Keoki and Kelolo, and her half-sister, Luka, did their best to comfort her, as did her stepmother, Llani, who could thus ease her own sorrow at the loss of a beloved husband by consoling the girl she loved as dearly as she did her own offspring.

Aukele wept too, because her grandfather had been so good and kind to her and because she saw her mother weeping. At seven, the little girl had inherited her mother's slim gracefulness and glossy black hair, but her intense blue eyes and sensitive mouth were her father's. Milliama had industriously taught her English, and only at bedtime when she told the child stories from the legends of Hawaii had she used the Hawaiian words. Aukele knew many of these, of course, but her mother was determined that the little girl should be given the fine education of a *haole*. And whenever her half-brothers or Luka visited the house on Waimanalo Beach, Milliama had insisted that they speak only in English before Aukele.

Luka, nearly twenty, was married to Hanale, a twenty-seven-year-old islander who worked in the big sugar-cane plantation at Ewa. Kalaiki had made Luka and Hanale the gift of an acre of land farther down along the beach at the time of Luka's marriage two years ago. And Milliama had given her half-sister some of the money still remaining in the bank to help out when Hanale and the other workers had gone out on strike last summer. Luka had her mother's buxom figure and genial nature, and because thus far she and Halane had not been blessed with offspring, she adored Aukele and was forever bringing her presents. One week there would be an exquisite necklace of shells that she had pierced and strung herself; another, a tiny little catamaran cut out of *koa* wood by Hanale. Milliama was even closer to Luka than to her stepmother, Llani, and the two young women confided in each other as all over the world young married women are wont to do. As August waned and the time for Aukele's going back to grammar school grew nearer, Milliama felt a strange and terrifying premonition, the same she had had at the cemetery. And that was why she told Luka, "My husband, Philip, has kin in San Francisco who have already written to me asking to adopt Aukele. If anything should happen to me, Luka, you must promise that you will let them know so that they may give Aukele a home. It is good that she grows up with her own people."

"You should not speak so, Milliama, it will bring bad luck," Luka chided. "You have mourned for your *haole* husband long enough. It is time, truly, my sister, that you take another man and give Aukele a father who will love her as Hanale and I love her."

But Milliama shook her head. "You know that I will not marry again, Luka. Let us not speak of that again, my sister. I know that Llani or you would take Aukele, but I think that Philip would want his child to be brought up with those relatives in San Francisco who have children of their own and would be able to give her so many things that I cannot. And she should live on the mainland so that when she is grown and a woman, she will understand how it is there as well as on the islands. You will do this for me if anything happens, Luka?"

"Of course, Milliama. But nothing is going to happen."

"It is well to be prepared for the future, just the same, Luka," Milliama persisted. "In the drawer of the secretary which is in Philip's room, there are the letters from his kinfolk. It has their address in San Francisco, and you must promise that you will tell them if I am taken from Aukele."

Tears came to Luka's eyes as she looked at the lovely, grave face of her half-sister. She bit her lips, then nodded and embraced Milliama. "You do not need to ask, my sister," she whispered.

"But this house and the land it is on and this beautiful beach, they will always belong to Aukele," Milliama resumed. "I have told you of the conch shell and how Philip put the paper which tells how this place is ours into it and buried it beneath the big papaya tree. No one but Aukele is to have the house and the land, Luka. I cannot leave her so much money or such nice things as Philip did, for I must work as I have done to make enough for Aukele's food and clothes, as well as her school and the books she must have. So, Luka, promise me that no matter what happens, you will not tell anyone about the conch shell. I myself will tell Aukele about it one day so that after I am gone, she will know how her father planned for her and for me."

"I will tell no one, if that is your wish, Milliama," Luka softly answered. . . .

And then, one night early in November, after Milliama had given her last show at the Kon-Tiki, Lee Wong, one of the co-owners of the cabaret, knocked at the door of her dressing room. "Mebbe you wait and not go home right now, Milliama," he anxiously exclaimed when she had opened the door to him.

"Why, what's wrong, Mr. Lee?" she asked, her beautiful dark eyes widening with surprise.

"Not so good." The little Chinese shook his head. "Two Filipino boys, good customers, they get drunk, say they both going take you out tonight. Mebbe you stay here till I call cops."

But Milliama knew that Llani or Luka were up late nearly every night watching over Aukele whenever she worked at the cabaret, and she was eager to get home to her daughter. She had bought a second-hand Ford for a few hundred dollars and drove to and from the cabaret whenever she worked. And there had been drunken customers before who loudly argued about taking her out after the show, sometimes interrupting the performance with their heckling and lewd expressions of desire for her. There was no reason to delay her getting back home tonight just because of what Lee Wong had told her. So she reassured the worried little Chinese and told him that she would be all right and that she would leave by the side entrance.

It had been raining most of that day, and the air was damp and there was no moon in the sky as she emerged onto the narrow sidestreet. It was a matter of walking round the block to where her car was parked, and then she soon would be home with Aukele. As she rounded the corner, two men jostled her. One of them stepped back, staggering a little as he lit a cigarette, and by the light of the match he recognized her. "You real nice *wahine*. I take you out and show you good time. You come with Santiago," he shouted, grabbing her by the wrist. But the other Filipino struck at him with his fist. "You wrong, de *wahine* rather go with Rinaldo. Hey, honey, I show you real good time, you see."

Milliama turned to run, but the wiry young Filipino named Santiago seized her by the shoulders, grinning owlishly. "You take your dirty hands off that *wahine*, Santiago, she gonna go wid me!" the stockier, older youth cried out.

"Let go of me, you're both drunk, I don't go out with customers!" Milliama gasped, trying to free herself. Rinaldo drew a knife and crept toward his crony. Santiago, seeing the danger, turned, pulling Milliama with him. Rinaldo had already started his vicious lunge with the knife, which sank deep into Milliama's back. Realizing what he had done, Milliama's assailant turned and ran down the street. Sobered and terror-stricken, Santiago let go of her, and the young woman slumped to the sidewalk, unconscious.

Chapter
FIVE

MILLIAMA MASON died the next morning without re-
gaining consciousness. Her half-sister, Luka, who had
waited all night long at the house on Waimanalo Beach
for her to return, had fallen asleep long after having put
Aukele to bed. There was a lounge chair on the veranda,
and Luka had gone out to relax and look at the ocean
and the sky at night. When Milliama had failed to return at her usual time, Luka had been greatly concerned, for her half-sister's fatalistic remarks about turning Aukele over to Philip Mason's kin in San Francisco
came back to mind and haunted her with a strange premonition of disaster.

She woke to see a man in uniform bending over her
and shaking her shoulder, and she uttered a cry of terror.
"Don't be afraid, I am a policeman," the man said to her.
Luka rose from the chair, her blood congealing with a
terrible presentiment. He was a heavyset, swarthy man
in the uniform of a Honolulu police officer, with ser-
geant's stripes. "What is wrong? Please tell me," Luka
gasped.

"Is this the house where Milliama Mason lives?" the
policeman asked. He held a red cloth purse, which Luka
at once recognized as Milliama's.

"Yes, this is her house. I am Luka, her half-sister, and
I look after her little girl, Aukele, when she works at the
Kon-Tiki. But what is the matter? How did you get her
purse?"

The policeman lowered his eyes and shifted uncomfortably. "There was a fight outside in the street," he explained. "Two Filipinos, who'd watched your sister dance, wanted her to go out with them. They quarreled, and one of them drew a knife. The other one was holding your sister, and to get away from the knife, he turned her toward it. She was stabbed, and she is now in the hospital. It is very serious, I am sorry to tell you."

"Poor Milliama! Please, can you take me with you to see her? We don't have a car. My husband, Hanale, gets a ride over to Ewa, where he works, but we don't own a car. I want to see Milliama, please!"

"Of course. I will drive you there."

"Wait just a minute, I'll get Aukele."

"I don't know if it's a good idea to let the little girl know about her mother, not something like this." Again the policeman shifted uncomfortably and looked away from Luka, his voice rough with compassion. "We arrested both men, but it was such a stupid thing, such a tragic thing. The manager of the cabaret, Lee Wong, testified that he urged your sister to stay in her dressing room till he could get the Filipinos away. As a matter of fact, he called the police, and that was how we happened to catch them both just after your sister was stabbed."

"She wanted to get back home to her daughter, that's why she wouldn't wait." Luka burst into tears.

She hurried back into the house and brought out the little girl, who rubbed her eyes with sleep and asked in a drowsy voice, "Luka, is it time to get up? I'm still so sleepy."

The big policeman scowled, took off his cap, scratched his thick black hair, replaced the cap, and tugged the visor down with a grimace that hid his mixed feelings. He eyed Luka, muttering, "I got two kids myself. Damn shame the little girl has to be brought into this *pilikia*."

Luka stiffened, her head proudly high. "Trouble? This little girl already has *pilikia* enough, Mr. Policeman. Her daddy was a *haole* schoolteacher, and he got killed

38

on Pearl Harbor Day. She didn't even get a chance to say goodbye to him. Her mother is her life. Sure I take her to see Milliama. Let's go now."

The little Japanese nurse who had let Luka and Aukele into the hospital room where Milliama lay after the transfusion that had been given her in the operating room turned away and dabbed at her eyes to hide her tears. The doctor had told Luka that Milliama had lost too much blood and that the transfusion was the last hope, for the knife had reached a vital spot. And when Luka had told him how Philip Mason had died and how Aukele worshipped her mother, he had told the nurse to let them in, but only for a few minutes.

Luka bent and kissed Milliama's cheek, while Aukele stared with wide, uncomprehending eyes at her unconscious mother. The pallor of approaching death had made Milliama's lovely face a classic cameo, capturing all the gentle beauty of spirit and flesh in unforgettable perfection. Luka had explained to Aukele, "Your mother is very sick, Aukele. But you must pray for her, and you must be a big, brave girl and not cry when you see her. You must remember her always as she was with you, happy and laughing and tender." And the little girl had seemed to understand, though she cuddled close to her aunt, her lips trembling but managing to suppress the sobs that surged to her throat. And when all hope was gone and the nurse closed Milliama's eyelids, Luka hugged the little girl and chokingly whispered, "You must be very brave. She has gone to live with your daddy now, in the bright heaven way up in the blue sky, and they will be very happy, and they will look down and see you all of your life, Aukele."

Luka had remembered her half-sister's last words to her, and Milliama's death had made those words a solemn edict, to be obeyed regardless of Luka's own desires. Though she had often told her husband, Hanale, that it would be a joy to have Aukele in their house and loved as their own child, now it was not to be. And that was why Luka had taken the letters of Dan Mason from the drawer of the secretary, learned the address of Philip Mason's cousin in San Francisco, and sent him a telegram about Milliama's death. Two days later, he arrived on the China Clipper and took a taxi to Luka's house.

It was morning, and Hanale was working in the fields at Ewa. Luka was reading from the Bible to Aukele, for she knew that Milliama had often read verses to the child just before bedtime. She had just begun the beautiful psalm "The Lord is my shepherd, I shall not want," when she heard the sound of footsteps and the knock at the door. She closed the Bible with trembling hands, knowing that the time had come to say farewell to Aukele, perhaps forever.

Philip Mason's younger cousin had just turned forty. He was of slightly more than medium height, stocky of build, with thinning black hair that already showed touches of gray at the temples. His face was rounded, with a hint of fleshly indulgence in the thick jowls and plump cheeks and the full, sensuous mouth. He wore a pince-nez over the bridge of a sharply hawklike nose, and his gray-blue eyes were close-set.

He wore an expensive tailored suit and a Panama hat and, out of a kind of vain fastidiousness, a pair of spats on his gleaming shoes. Luka studied him attentively. He was undoubtedly the kind of *haole* who had money, she decided. That was good, for Milliama had wanted Aukele to have every advantage on the mainland. Yet money could not buy the serenity and beauty that were here on the island where Pele had once made her home, where there had once been a great warrior race and many mighty kings and princesses. There was still the blood of the islands in Aukele's veins, the inheritance of Milliama, who had been the daughter of Kalaiki, once a chief on a distant island and perhaps himself descended from great kings of the ancient past. And with that blood, Aukele could never forget Hawaii. Yet if she did —Luka took comfort in the thought—the house on Waimanalo Beach was hers by legacy of birth.

She kissed the little girl, whom she had dressed in the very best clothes Aukele owned. The child's other things had been neatly packed in a large cardboard box. "You must go with him, Aukele," she said to the little girl. "He is of your father's family, and he has children with whom you can play and be happy."

Aukele clung to Luka, shrinking back against the buxom young woman, her eyes frightened. "But I don't want to leave you, Luka!" she exclaimed. "I want to stay in the house on the beach. I want to stay here with you and Llani and Keoki and Kelolo. Please let me stay here, Luka!"

Dan Mason uneasily cleared his throat. "You'll see them again," he promised. "We have a big house in San Francisco, Aukele—by the way, Luka, is that really the name Philip Mason gave the girl? Back in San Francisco, it'll sound odd when she goes to school."

"It is the Hawaiian name for Audrey, Mr. Mason," Luka replied coolly. Already the distress of parting from Aukele grieved her, and now this casual remark about Milliama's daughter's name made her uneasy, as if she felt that life would be changed in many ways for the little girl. "Milliama told me that her husband had a little sister who died, and that it was in her memory that he named his daughter."

"Then we'll call her Audrey. She speaks excellent English, and so do you, Luka," Dan Mason smiled ingratiatingly as he picked up the box of the little girl's belongings.

"Did you expect us to be savages, Mr. Mason?" Luka's voice was defiant and her eyes flashed with indignation. "Milliama was a pupil at McKinley, where your cousin taught school. She was very bright, and she made good grades, and he fell in love with her. And I myself have gone to school. Of course it is true that Milliama taught Aukele"—she flung the child's name back at him with a kind of challenge—"many words that we use on the island. There is nothing wrong in that."

"Of course not, Luka; of course not," Dan Mason

soothed her. "I didn't mean to offend you, Luka. Of course you're not a savage. It's only that children in the States sometimes poke fun at their schoolmates who have unusual names or come from a distant place. Now, there's something I must ask you which has to do with the estate."

"Estate?" Luka echoed uncomprehendingly.

"I mean," he amended, "surely my cousin left some money in the bank for Milliama. Since the child's parents are both dead now, she inherits the money. But since she is not of age, and I will be her guardian and foster-parent, the law says that I may take this money and use it for her schooling and her care."

"I understand now. Yes, it is true, Milliama showed me the bankbook. I suppose you will know how to get the money, but it is for Aukele, remember that!" Again, Luka could not suppress the impulse to protect the little girl who was so dear to her.

"Of course. I shall go with the child to a lawyer in Honolulu and arrange for the transfer of the money to the mainland. It will be in a bank in her name, and if there is any left when she comes of age, of course she will have it."

Luka nodded silently. Then, remembering the house on the beach, she said, "There is a home to which she can return when she misses the island too much, Mr. Mason. Milliama's husband bought the land on the beach from my father, who helped him build his house there. Milliama has told me many times that the land and the house belong to Aukele. It is so written."

"I understand that too. But there will be taxes on this house and this land, and I will pay them every year so that the property does not become forfeit. In that way, you see, Luka, it will be the property of Aukele always."

"That is very good, Mr. Mason. Aukele, you must go with him now. You have already said your goodbyes to Llani and my brothers. Come—we will say our last goodbye in the garden." She turned to Dan Mason and added in a beseeching tone, "You will let us say goodbye in our own garden by ourselves, please, Mr. Mason?"

"You mean in the garden back of Philip's house? Of course, if you wish, Luka. I have a taxi waiting outside. It'll take you and the child there, and afterwards she and I'll go back to Honolulu. I'll take her with me to some of the shops I have to visit, and then tonight we'll fly back to San Francisco," Dan Mason explained.

A few minutes later, while the cab waited out on the dirt road, Luka led the little girl by the hand, while Dan Mason carried the big cardboard box. It was only a mile or two to the house with the cupola and the spired weathervane, and the day was bright and warm. The ocean had never seemed bluer or more placid than on this day when Aukele Mason, daughter of Philip and Milliama Mason, was about to bid it farewell.

"Take as long as you want, Luka," Dan Mason said, clearing his throat again to hide the embarrassment of being an intruder on this intimate scene of parting. "I'll just smoke a cigarette or two and relax. We've plenty of time."

"Thank you." Luka inclined her head. Her bearing was one of dignified coolness as she got out of the cab and helped Aukele down. They walked from the dirt road over the little dune and toward the wire that enclosed the spacious garden extending for hundreds of feet beyond the two-story house. Atop the spire, the weathervane pointed in the direction of the gentle trade-wind. Luka opened the little gate, and she and Aukele walked down the winding path where Philip Mason and Milliama had walked so often to admire the magnificent tropical splendor of their vast garden. Here were orange trumpet vines, the *huapala*, which means "sweetheart" in Hawaiian, with their long, slender, tubelike flowers from which four or five lobes curled gently back. And here were the cream and rose oleander flowers tipping the branches of ten-foot-high shrubs, and there were bushes of the pale reddish-orange blossoms of the ixora, whose bushes towered fifteen feet high, with their groups of four-petaled flowers forming a dazzling ball of riotous color. Farther on, as they neared the back of the house,

43

there were clumps of *hau* trees, and Luka's father had planted them so that the branches interlocked and formed a roof overhead, a kind of little summer house for Milliama and her *haole* husband. They had gnarled trunks several feet thick, and their flowers were bright yellow with a dark throat at the center. Luka paused here and bit her lips in sorrowful recollection, knowing how Milliama had loved this sheltered retreat. The blossoms of the *hau*, yellow at the beginning of the day, turned to apricot color; and by nightfall when they were ready to drop, they became a deep red. All the magic of Hawaii seemed incarnate here in this shady enclosure.

There were patches of the *oliwa-ku-kahaki*, the beech oleanders with their curiously shaped pinkish-green balloonlike cylinders growing in a tall spike from the center of the plant. And there was the yellow allamanda, those large, velvety, golden-yellow flowers flourishing from sprawling vines, with their smooth, thick, pointed leaves, as well as the night-blooming cereus, whose huge buds open about eight o'clock at night between June and October. Still closer to the back of the house were rows of yellow ginger plants, with their exquisitely fragrant light yellow blossoms, rising from the end of narrow tubes of olive-colored bracts, and close to them the pinkish sheath of the heliconia, with its yellow and green edging.

And then, just in back of the house, there was a circular clearing in which Kalaiki had planted five papaya trees; in the center, the tallest rose twenty feet high, fruit clustering under its branches. The other four that circled it were from a dozen to fifteen feet in height. Luka drew Aukele toward the center of this clearing. "These are the good-luck trees your grandfather Kalaiki planted before you were born, *hiwahiwa*," she said tenderly to the little girl. And that endearment, which means "precious" in Hawaiian, brought tears to her eyes again at the thought of abandoning Milliama's daughter to this stranger. "Always remember this tree among all others, Aukele. You must promise me something and swear it by the names of your father and mother."

"What must I swear, Luka?"

"That you will keep this secret and tell it to no one, no, not even to this man who will take you to the mainland, Aukele. It is your secret, and Philip, your father, and Milliama, your mother, wished it to be thus. Will you promise this?"

The little girl nodded solemnly, squeezing Luka's hand in an access of emotion that she herself did not fully comprehend.

"Under this big tree, Aukele, there is buried a conch shell. Your father found it on the beach. Into it he put the paper which says that this beautiful garden and this house and the beach beyond to the ocean waves themselves shall belong to you forever, Aukele. You must never let anyone else have them, for they belong to you. Do you understand?"

"Yes, Luka. Will I come back to see you very soon? And see Llani and Keoki and Kelolo and Hanale, too?"

"He says that he will bring you back, Aukele. I pray that that will be so, for you are like my own daughter, *hiwahiwa*. But one day, if he should not bring you here, your *hoku*—your star of fate—will bring you back to the island. Remember that always, Aukele. And now, we must say goodbye until we meet again. *A hui hou haua*, my darling one! Till we meet again!"

Chapter
SIX

IT WAS an old house, and it had survived the great San Francisco earthquake of 1906, though the fire that followed the earthquake had very nearly reached it. It stood on Lombard Street, a narrow and winding thoroughfare that ascended its tortuous way up gradual hills. It was on the corner of Hyde, and only a few blocks westward, Lombard terminated in a dead end, a circular rise from which one could see the Golden Gate Bridge to the north. At night, especially when the fog rolled in from Seal Rock, creeping at first stealthily over the outer edge of Golden Gate Park and then, gathering density and momentum, rolling boldly over the entire park and embracing the old streets like Lombard, as well as the newer Marina district, there was a ghostlike atmosphere to its old cobblestones and cracked pavements and twisted curbs. Even the old metal lampposts, with their huge opaque glass bulbs sending a weird glow through the ectoplasm of fog, took on the character of props at a medium's seance when the black of night and the thick gray of fog coalesced.

The house itself was two stories high, but with the illusion of three given it by an ingeniously devised mansard roof that sloped on both sides to allow for the receding dormers that had been originally constructed as attic storage rooms. They had casement windows, gloomy and forbidding as soon as the sun set, and even during bright daylight not always illumined by the sun, because the other houses along the ascending street diverted its rays. There was a wide porch supported by four columns, and seven wide, heavy wooden steps led to it. An old iron picket fence thrust its grim barrier around the house and the little garden behind it, as if its occupants wished no communication with the somewhat more recently built house next door. The fence had been painted several times, yet still managed to look rusty and old—the corrosive effect of fog and rain and wind over the years. Along the sides of the house, long, twisting vines of dark green ivy clambered nearly to the second floor, and at the base of the house thick growths of moss and lichen had become so dense that they seemed a very part of the foundation itself.

The turret of the mansard roof was suggested in the way the roof of the porch slanted, so that rain would be directed away from it. As one walked slowly up Lombard Street, the house seemed to perch at an angle, staunch in its solidarity, its angular chimney rising at the back as if to arch the edifice higher than its neighbors to the east. And at the back of the house, in the garden, stood eucalyptus and pine trees, while the wall that faced the rising sun and enclosed the cheery, old-fashioned, roomy kitchen swarmed with curling arbutus and the triangulated dark green moss of ivy leaves, intertwining. Dan Mason had even imported a gingko tree at the very back of the garden, rising above a stone birdbath that had been there since he had acquired the house and yet to which no birds flocked because it held water only when the rain fell. Margery Mason detested birds because "they're so messy and noisy." So, although Grover and Beatrice might have enjoyed making pets of the sparrows or the pigeons or the gulls, their parents did not encourage such an inclination.

The house had once been a gleaming white; now, it was a morose gray, and it looked gloomy and deserted when the first darkening of twilight banished the sun along Lombard Street. It had always been a quiet residential street, and one seldom heard the laughter of children. Margery Mason herself had taken pains in her rearing of Grover and Beatrice so that they would be quiet children, not given to the shrill screeching so often heard during children's games nor the irritating running back and forth over the heavily beamed floors of the old house. Dan's father had rented the place from a retired fishing-schooner captain whose acumen and skill at making friends had enabled him to induce some of his less fortunate labor fishermen to work for him. The captain had made a contract with a popular seafood restaurant at Fisherman's Wharf to provide crabs and abalone and sea bass, and he had made a fortune. Later, he had decided to sell the house to Dan's father for a good deal less than what it would be worth on the market today. The taxes were considerable, but the house was an inheritance along with the import shop on O'Farrell Street.

And it was to this house on a dreary, rainy November evening that Dan Mason brought little Aukele in a cab that had taken them from the airport along the picturesque road that led from South San Francisco through Westlake and then Nineteenth Avenue. Aukele Mason had sat entranced, peering out the window, her hands tightly clasped in her lap as the city unfolded before her. Dan Mason thought to himself that the trip by plane from Honolulu and now this cab ride had been exactly the right prescription to divert the child's mind from leaving Luka and her dead mother. There would have to be a great many changes in the child's education, to be sure. You could hardly expect schools on that Godforsaken island where once savages had lived and made human sacrifices to a volcano goddess named Pele to compare in any way with the fine elementary and high schools of San Francisco. And the next thing to do was to get her decent clothes. This gaudy, loose thing she wore, which Luka had called a *muu-muu* was certainly out of the question in a respectable city. All she wore under it was a kind of tiny petticoat. Margery would have a fit. But what else could you expect of a dreamy idealist like his cousin Philip, who had got himself trapped into mar-

49

rying some flirtatious native girl and then decided to shuck everything and live there the rest of his life? In a way, Dan Mason righteously thought to himself, he was performing a very creditable act of charity in taking the child away from that plump young Hawaiian woman Luka, who probably would have fed the kid nothing but coconuts and pineapple and that nauseating *poi*. He had had a taste of it, and it had reminded him of library paste. He grimaced at the recollection.

"Uncle Dan, aren't there any palm trees here?" Aukela was asking him. On the plane, he had told her that it would be nice if she would call him Uncle Dan instead of Cousin Dan. It would sound more like a parent, because at forty he hardly considered himself a cousin to this winsome child. She was a strange one, all right, but one thing in her favor was that she could be quiet for quite a long spell. He wondered what was going on in her head all the time and how she would adapt herself to growing up with Grover and Beatrice.

The cab stopped in front of the old house, and Dan Mason got out and helped Aukele out to the sidewalk. "Careful now, dear," he cautioned. "It's very hilly and you mustn't try to run or play until you know what it's like."

"Oh, but I like hills, Uncle Dan," Aukele responded in her sweet, clear voice. "Can you see the ocean from this house, Uncle Dan?"

"Yes, sometimes from the garden on a clear day. And you can see the Bay Bridge from the attic room at the top of the house," he explained as he paid and tipped the driver. Then, picking up the cardboard box containing Aukele's belongings by the heavy cord that had been carefully tied around it, he took her by the hand and led her up the steps of the house. "Oh, it's like a tower room up there, isn't it, Uncle Dan?" Aukele joyously exclaimed. "Just like Daddy's tower. Maybe I can see the ocean from there, Uncle Dan. Will you let me?"

"Come along, Audrey, it's past your bedtime as it is.

We'll talk about it tomorrow. Besides, I want you to meet your new cousins Grover and Beatrice and your Aunt Margery. They've been looking forward to meeting you, Audrey."

The little girl, wearing the light cloth coat Dan Mason had bought her at a shop in the airport building to ward off the foggy chill of a San Francisco night, straightened and let go of his hand, looking at him with burnished blue eyes and the nuance of a wistful tremor at her sensitive mouth. "My name is Aukele, Uncle Dan. My daddy and mummy called me that all the time, and so did Luka."

"Yes, yes, I know," Dan Mason said impatiently as he rang the doorbell. "But that's the Hawaiian name for Audrey, and now that you're going to live with us, you'll have to get used to answering to Audrey from now on, do you understand, dear? It means the same thing, you know."

"Yes, Mummy told me it did," the little girl stubbornly insisted, "and I was called after Daddy's sister who died when she was a little girl, too. But isn't it just as easy for my new cousins and my aunt and you to call me Aukele, Uncle Dan?"

His face tightened with annoyance, but before he could answer, the door was opened by Margery Mason. At thirty-four, the blond socialite was still attractive, but the sharpness of her features had been accentuated by the years and by the economic tensions the Mason household had endured during the war because of the decline of Dan's import business. Her eyes were blue, though they were a lighter shade than Aukele's, and they were closely set together beside the bridge of an aristocratic but somewhat exaggeratedly aquiline nose whose thin, flaring nostrils could very eloquently express disdain or disapproval. Her face might have been an admirable cameo were it not for this flaw and the somewhat angular prominence of a determined chin, as well as her small and rather thin-lipped mouth. She was rather

51

tall, about five feet eight inches, elegantly slim, and immaculately gowned. At the sight of the china-blue silk dress with its puffed sleeves, his particular favorite, Dan Mason's face lost the irritated look the little girl's insistence had aroused. He put down the cardboard box just inside the door, turned, and drew Aukele over the threshold of her new home, then took his wife in his arms and kissed her. "Here's Audrey home at last, darling," he told her.

"My name is Aukele," the slim, black-haired child repeated, and now her lips were noticeably trembling and her eyes were blinking quickly with the first tears of homesickness and separation from kindly Luka. Now the anguish for her dead mother welled up in her heart, and she burst into tears, ashamed of herself for behaving so badly in front of strangers and yet unable to suppress her sobs.

Margery Mason drew a deep breath and shook her head. "There's no need to cry, Audrey." Her voice was briskly impersonal. "You'll be happy here. And you'll have lots more fun, because you'll have cousins of your own to play with. Come along, child. You'll find Beatrice and Grover waiting for you in the living room to welcome you."

With an effort, Aukele controlled her sobs, sniffled, and then straightened. "I'm sorry, Aunt Margery. I didn't mean to cry. I'm ready now."

"That's a good child." Margery Mason smiled. "Come along, then."

Dan Mason closed the door behind him and followed Margery and the little girl into the huge living room. Grover, eight years old, towheaded and already showing his father's stockiness of build, and Beatrice, the same age as her cousin, with two thick coppery pigtails and a pert, sulky face, obediently rose from the ornate and overstuffed horsehair sofa on which they had been waiting. It was far past their bedtime, but Margery Mason had permitted this dispensation in view of the extraordinary circumstances of the occasion. Besides, tomorrow was Saturday, there was no school, and they could sleep late. She beamed as she saw them rise in unison. They were such well-behaved, intelligent children. Almost precocious, indeed, judging from the midterm report cards they had so proudly brought her just the other day.

"Children, this is your little cousin Audrey." She put one arm around Aukele and with the other made an ostentatious gesture, almost like that of a Roman matron summoning her slaves. "She is going to live here with us from now on. Audrey, dear, say hello to Beatrice."

"How do you do, Beatrice?" Aukele solemnly pronounced.

At this, the red-haired child tossed her head till her pigtails danced and replied in a thin, reedy voice, "So you're why we got to stay up so late tonight, huh?"

"Beatrice Mason!" Margery Mason sternly reproved this breach of etiquette. "That's not at all nice, and you know it isn't. Now, say what I taught you to say to your cousin, dear."

Beatrice made an impish face at Aukele. Her mother frowned and added, "Now, now, dear, that won't do at all. You'd like to go to the movie tomorrow afternoon with Grover, wouldn't you?"

"Oh, sure, Mama. I forgot. I'm sorry." Beatrice came forward, held out her hand to Aukele, and said, in the voice of one who recites a lesson, "I'm happy to know you, Audrey. We shall have lots of fun together playing games, shan't we? I hope you had a nice trip." She then stepped back to her place in front of the sofa, looking to her mother for applause.

Margery Mason turned to her husband with a doting smile. "Isn't that sweet, Dan? Now then, Grover dear, it's your turn."

The towheaded youngster walked slowly forward, his somewhat astigmatic hazel eyes squinting at Aukele, whose light coat did not cover the loose, wide skirt of the orange, red, and yellow *muu-muu* nor her bare feet

53

thrust into thong sandals. Then he irreverently sniggered, "My gosh, all she's got on's a nightie? Is that all they wear where she comes from, Daddy?"

Aukele Mason drew back with a gasp, her creamy tan skin reddening with humiliation. Then, goaded by the mocking face of the boy as much as by his taunt, she slapped him, burst into tears, and ran out of the room, hysterically crying, "I want to go back home to Luka! I don't want to stay here, I don't, I don't!"

Chapter
SEVEN

JUST AS Philip Mason had intended to stay only a little while in Oahu and found the weeks stretching into years, so his daughter, Aukele—now known as Audrey—managed to overcome her loneliness and homesickness that first November night and to grow up in the old house on Lombard Street. Dan and Margery Mason had at first regretted their impulsive generosity in offering to bring up the little girl whom Dan had brought back to San Francisco after her mother's tragic death. The first few months were trying, indeed, but more so for the child than for her new parents, for such they now were. It seemed to her that in denying her the right to be called by the Hawaiian name with which Philip and Milliama Mason had endowed her, she was being made to feel like a probationer, like someone who did not belong to the well-ordered little world in which Dan and Margery Mason and their two children lived.

Nor did she at once forget the humiliating jibe with which thoughtless little Grover had first greeted her. Used to the warm sun and the lush verdure and the blazing multicolored floral glory of the island on which she had been born, she at first hated the fogginess and the comparatively desolate atmosphere of the neighborhood in which she was now obliged to live. Yet because innately she had much of her mother's sweet docility, she quickly learned to adapt herself to the regimen of the Mason household. Milliama had urged her always to study diligently whatever lessons she was given at school, and Margery Mason wisely decided to enroll her in the nearby grammar school right after the Christmas holidays, thereby giving Audrey well over a month in which to adjust herself to this strange new life. And to her credit, it must be said that Margery Mason dispensed with many of her social appointments during that time, spending several afternoons a week taking Audrey sightseeing to the Fleishhacker Zoo, to Seal Rock, and to the picturesque waterfront shops, so that Audrey would become more familiar with the colorful and exciting facets of this city on the mainland which was now her home. Wisely, too, she took Grover and Beatrice along on as many of these excursions as their own school schedule permitted, to accustom them to their new cousin and playmate. And that first Christmas away from Hawaii, Audrey was given fully as many gaily wrapped gifts as Grover and Beatrice to show her that she was henceforth to be on an equal footing with them and to have no fewer privileges or tokens of the Masons' regard.

The first few weeks in school were, to be sure, difficult for Philip's little daughter, for she still occasionally lapsed into Hawaiian phrases when these best expressed what she wished to say. Conversely, her aptitude for learning and her diligence delighted her teachers, who fortunately were sensitive to her need for acceptance, recognition, and affection. And thus gradually the transition was made. From secret derision at this newcomer in their midst, her classmates soon passed to grudging admiration and then envy at her bright mind and excellent grades. And Audrey's charming sincerity helped lull even that envy into genuine admiration, for often a child, better than any adult, can sense when one of his fellows seeks the spotlight of attention and adulation. Audrey accepted her teachers' praise with a meek pleasure that promptly disarmed them, as well as her classmates.

She had her own room on the second floor of the old house on Lombard Street, but often she would climb the winding stairway to the dormer just above the second floor and spend many a long hour staring out the window. Sometimes she would close her eyes and pretend that she could see the bright blue ocean and the shimmering white sand of the beach that stretched beyond the house where she and her father and mother had lived. And when she opened her eyes, it was always with a sigh of disappointment that only the houses across the street and, in the distance, the hilly angle of the street as it labored upward to the dead-end clearing were in view. Sometimes, on a particularly clear day, by straining her eyes and looking toward the east, she could catch a glimpse of the structure of the winding Bay Bridge, which led to Oakland, and it almost seemed that she could see the stretch of water that it spanned. Again, Margery Mason proved perceptive in realizing how much the little girl might miss the beauty of that island, and when she learned that Audrey had been swimming a great deal with her mother, she proposed to her husband that Audrey, Beatrice, and Grover spend an occasional hour over a weekend swimming in one of the heated pools in the Marina or Geary districts. Dan Mason, busier than ever with the problem of keeping his import shop on O'Farrell Street in the black, gave his wife a free hand in rearing Audrey. He was not by nature an outwardly affectionate man, though he preferred his son Grover to Beatrice simply because Grover represented the heir who would succeed him and take over his business when the time came.

The import business was one of varying fortune, depending on the influx of goods that would catch the eye of the regular patron and tourist alike. It took good judgment to decide what items should be stocked and to anticipate the customer trend. One year, exquisitely inlaid little spice boxes proved to be greatly in demand; the very next year, they gathered dust on the shelves. And there was serious competition, too, from Gump's and Cost Plus Imports. They advertised a good deal more than he did, and besides the entire city was changing.

Dan Mason prided himself on being a native San Franciscan, and like many such, he longed for the "good old days" just before the war, when business had been booming and the still liberal political regime had looked the other way so far as fleshpots were concerned. Of course, it hadn't been like the historical old Barbary Coast, and nothing would ever bring that back. But just the same, San Francisco had been a free and easygoing city where wine, women, and song were readily available to those who could pay the price. The tourists had come in droves. Many of them had decided to live in San Francisco permanently, and the money they spent had benefited the merchants of the city.

But gradually that was all changing, and he wasn't happy about it. The mayor and the chief of police had been clamping down on some of the nightclubs, and many a conventioneer who had visited his shop had told him that it wasn't so easy to find a girl any more. Dan Mason was a pragmatist; though he himself was rigidly faithful to his marital vows, he nonetheless had a practical business philosophy when it came to his own shop and those conditions which could affect it for better or for worse. His motto was, "Leave things as they are and don't drive away the tourists by bluenosing." And yet he could see it happening already. If it kept up, the conventioneers and the tourists would pick Los Angeles and spend their dollars there instead of in San Francisco and in his shop.

Beatrice and Audrey went on to the same high school, in the same class. Dan's red-haired daughter had never readily accepted Audrey and throughout their childhood had maintained an attitude of merely tolerating the slim brunet girl as a playmate when no one else was available. She resented Audrey's intrusion into the household, because it detracted from the attention she felt was her rightful due. In grammar school, she had felt embarrassed many times when her friends had maliciously poked fun at Audrey's ridiculously perfect English tinged with the soft accent of the islands and at her creamy tan complexion, so often the mark of the Polynesian fusion

58

with Caucasian blood. Beatrice had found herself on the defensive, trying to explain Audrey's presence, and it irritated her. Sometimes, in vindictive retaliation, she would ignore her cousin for hours at a time or rudely refuse to answer some question about schoolwork or Audrey's friendly overtures to share some childhood game.

In high school, this hidden rancor lessened to an extent because Beatrice discovered that she had suddenly become attracted to the opposite sex. And, indeed, she was turning into an adolescent beauty by the time she reached her sophmore year. An inch taller than Audrey, with a fine, warmly tawny skin, full mouth, and highset cheekbones, she drew the notice of many of the appreciative young males at school, who clustered around her like bees around the hive, seeking to carry home her books or to buy her sodas and soft drinks at the campus sweetshop. Audrey, demure and quiet, made no attempt to rival Beatrice in this sudden blossoming, and so her red-haired cousin became more indulgent toward her.

The high school boasted an excellent swimming pool, and here Audrey spent many hours, both during her gym class and after school, swimming and diving. She found joy in this sport, just as she had as a child under Milliama's supervision on the white beach of Waimanalo. Beatrice, not to be outdone, often joined her when she was not busy with her newly found coterie of attentive young males. In their senior year, both girls were star members of the swimming team and helped win several victories over their high school's traditional rivals. Their coach, a former Olympic star now in his forties, was proud of having "discovered" two such promising swimmers and still more proud of the fine competitive record the team achieved, especially since the sports writers, who remembered him from his own stellar era, printed many complimentary items about Beatrice and Audrey. It was typical of Beatrice Mason that she kept a scrapbook and faithfully pasted into it every clipping that mentioned her prowess. Audrey had no particular interest in the sudden adulation her coach showed her; once in the water, it was as if she were a different person, transformed into the happy, carefree child who had fearlessly paddled out with her mother from the white-sanded beach of that island paradise. And when the coach intimated to her that she should go on with her swimming when she entered college and try to enter as many meets as possible, suggesting that she might even have a future on the Olympic team, Audrey laughed gently and replied, "To me, swimming is as natural as breathing, Mr. Johnson. It's pleasure for me, not work, and I'm afraid that thinking about meets and teams would take away from the pleasure. But it's very kind of you to say such nice things about me. Anyway, Beatrice is as good as I am."

But the coach had shaken his head and answered, "You're wrong, Audrey honey. Beatrice is flashy and very fast, that's true enough, but she doesn't have your stamina and poise. Take it from me, young lady, if you ever want to have a swimming career, you just have to work a little bit more and learn some of the tricks. And if you're in earnest about it at any time, I'll be very glad to help you all I can."

Meanwhile, Grover Mason was finding his own friends and interests throughout the formative years of high school. He too was adept in athletics, and his real fortes were baseball and football. He had inherited his father's sturdiness of build, though not the former's tendency to paunch and jowls. In high school, he made the all-city team as a defensive halfback and immediately found himself beseiged by admiring Lolitas who cheered his every play on the football field. Their squeals and shouts of encouragement urged him on to heroic prowess on the baseball diamond too, and it is recorded that his team lost the all-important final game of the season against its traditional rival, Granger High, as a result of Grover Mason's overflattered ego.

In the bottom half of the ninth inning, with Grover's team trailing by a run, Grover was perched on third base as a result of a triple. After the next batter struck out, Grover, inspired by the strident cries of encouragement from his feminine fans, tried to steal home and was ignominiously tagged out twenty feet away from scoring the tying run.

Upon Grover's graduation from high school, Dan bought his son a car, and Grover's preoccupation with the opposite sex grew apace. He squired one pretty teenager after another, glorying in showing her off to his less fortunate fellows, and twice received tickets for speeding. There followed a lengthy lecture from his father, but it was tempered with Dan's obvious affection for his only son and heir. After the lecture, Grover told his sister in Audrey's hearing, "Dad just has to show he's still head of the house, Bee. He really didn't bawl me out. Personally, I think he got a charge out of it."

The few thousand dollars that had been left in the Honolulu bank at the time of Milliama's death had long since been spent, though frugally, on Audrey's clothes and the nominal expenses a child's growing up occasions, such as dental care and the like. At the same time, each spring Dan Mason was reminded of his philanthropy in rearing Philip Mason's child by the tax bill forwarded to him from Honolulu. And where at about the time of the outbreak of the war the taxes had amounted to about $100, they had risen by 1959, the year of statehood for Hawaii to nearly $500 a year. With a dogged sense of conscience for his cousin's memory and the offer he himself had made to Milliama after Philip's death, Dan Mason paid those taxes, even though the past few years he had found it something of a hardship to meet that annual obligation. Nevertheless, in view of his paternal preference for Grover, he couldn't help thinking at times that the check he sent off to the Bureau of Conveyances on King Street could have gone instead to send Grover off to camp or to buy him a new wardrobe or to give him additional spending money for his pleasures.

The summer that saw Hawaii win statehood at last was an eventful one for Audrey. Margery Mason had had

61

an invitation from Sue Wells, who had been a sorority sister of hers and then married a famous portrait painter whose studio was near Santa Cruz. Sue invited Margery and her children to spend July and August at their huge, rambling, ranch-type house just off the beach, and Margery Mason readily accepted. Dan Mason, again concerned over the slack business of the import shop, declined the invitation with a sigh of relief; he welcomed the opportunity to devote all his time to the shop and to determining what steps he should take to improve its traffic and volume. Grover, who was in his junior year at San Francisco University (which both Beatrice and Audrey attended as sophomores), showed little enthusiasm for the offer, much to his mother's irritation, as Sue Wells was one of her oldest and dearest friends. The fact was, Grover Mason was already secretly embroiled with a vivacious and somewhat amoral freshman coed on whom he was spending a good deal of his time and a considerable part of his allowance, and the thought of being separated from her for two months was an irksome prospect. But the danger of alienating his mother, who naturally sided with him and often failed to tell his father about some of his extravagances, decided him to go along grudgingly with his sister and Audrey.

The night before their departure for Santa Cruz, Grover met Jessica Laswell and bade her a reluctant goodbye until the fall. Jessica was emotional, passionate, and ambitious; she saw in Grover a distinct catch, because judging by his elegant car, expensive wardrobe, and always-filled wallet, he would appear to come from a highly prosperous family, position in which would give her the security for which she strove. Her father had been a cable-car conductor, and her mother had worked in a laundry on Union Street. They had never had very much money. They lived in a squalid flat near the Fillmore District, and Jessica had never had the gewgaws and pretty dresses for which she had pined ever since her twelfth birthday, when her mother had taken her windowshopping at Blum's and told her that she would grow up to be a lovely young woman and one day should have all these fine things. Indeed, only her father's accidental death and the company's payment of a large compensation award together with his own group insurance had enabled her to go on from high school to the university.

For his part, Grover Mason thrilled to her extremely flattering attention and obvious awe of his own background, which he made seem more glamorous than it actually was. He had told her that his father ran a flourishing mercantile business—and he took pains to see that she never went near the crowded little shop on O'Farrell Street, lest she discover his deception. On the night of their parting for the summer, Jessica, swept away by her desire to trap him into marriage, yielded her virginity to him in a motel, and Grover swore undying pledges of eventual marriage, tempering these, however, with the admonition that they would both have to wait until after his graduation the following year.

Sue Wells, a homely, freckle-faced, lean woman in her late forties, warmly welcomed the Masons upon their arrival, as did her husband, Richard, a tall, genial-featured man with a shock of unruly gray hair and the vitality of a man of half his fifty years. Audrey, who had been hesitant about going along because she felt herself an intruder at the Wellses', took an immediate liking to the candid and friendly couple. And her hesitance in having gone along was immediately swept away when Richard Wells, at the dinner table, casually mentioned, "I don't know if you young people like to swim, but we've got some wonderful surfing out here along the coast. Maybe you'd like to try it. I think I could scare up a couple of extra boards if you would."

"Oh, that would be wonderful, Mr. Wells!" Audrey replied eagerly. "But I'm afraid that the only time I ever used a board was when I was a very little girl back in Honolulu. My mother got me a paddleboard, and of course, I didn't go out very far."

"Nonsense!" Richard Wells boomed encouragingly.

"From what I've heard about your swimming ability from your Aunt Margery, you'll take to it like a duck to water. Why don't we give it a try this afternoon?"

In a toolshed adjacent to the Wellses' garage, the genial artist had stacked several Malibu boards, with strong and dense foam. Quickly he explained the importance of the board in surfing to Beatrice, Audrey, and Grover. "You've got to choose a board with a good, solid stringer," Wells said. "It ought to be a good, solid strip of wood, though sometimes a good fiberglas will make up for it. And the skeg is pretty important, don't you ever forget it, because if it isn't secured properly to the tail of your board, it'll break off and you'll be in trouble. The skeg is to a board what a fin is to a fish, and probably the best material used in surfing is the all-fiberglas skeg. You see, it binds well, resists impact, and has plenty of strength. Your beaded wooden fins are pretty and all that, but they don't hold up half as well. Now let's go out and try the boards I've got here. We'll start real slow; you can't be an expert overnight."

"They're lovely," Audrey breathed, running her hand over the surface of one of the boards. "I sort of remember that mine was a rubber mat."

"Sure," Richard Wells agreed. "Some of today's top surfers had their first wave ride bouncing along on top of a rubber-canvas surf mat, and I'll bet that's what your mother got you back in Honolulu. There's some terrific surfing out there, not only at Waikiki Beach, but at Makaha, where they hold the championship meets. What I wouldn't give to go out there for all those meets! But I've got so darned many painting commissions, and we have to eat, so I have to content myself with Monterey Bay or once in a great while Malibu. Besides, Sue's sort of a hermit, and she's stuck on this location, so we spend most of our time around Santa Cruz."

The four of them carried their boards out to the sandy beach, and Richard Wells pointed out the slowly rolling waves. "Surfing is great in the early morning when your waves are smooth and the afternoon or evening winds don't ruffle them," he told his listeners. "One thing you'll have to get used to, Audrey, is the cold water. The temperature is pretty cold the year round, nothing like Hawaiian waters."

"I'm not afraid of cold water," Audrey laughed. "It's exhilarating and clean. Oh, those are beautiful waves out there!"

"That they are," Wells chuckled. "Well, why don't we paddle out and the three of you watch my stuff. Not that I'm a showoff, but I think I've done a little more surfing than any of the rest of you. Then you can try to get the feel of it yourself, that's the only way."

Holding their boards, the three young people watched the wiry gray-haired painter launch his board. There was a brief stretch of rocks off to the right, beyond which large waves could be seen gathering. Richard Wells turned his board upside-down to place the skeg in the air and keep from snagging on the way out, with the nose of the board up so that the gently rolling waves inward could not wrest it from his grip. Once he had cleared the rocks and got out into deep water, he clambered onto the board and stretched himself out over it, one leg bent at the knee and the foot sticking up in the air, his head up. Then he began a paddling armstroke, dipping his hands and arms in the water and pulling back and through, his fingers relaxed to reduce the tension.

"Gosh," Beatrice commented, "there's a technique even in getting out to the waves, isn't there?"

"Yes, there is," Audrey confirmed. "There was a book on surfing at the library in high school, I remember. It told how sometimes surfers take workouts of five miles or more, just paddling and getting their muscles in good condition. See how smoothly he's heading out to the waves!"

Grover was testing the water with his foot and scowling. "He sure is right about its being cold," he vouchsafed. "I think I prefer a heated pool back in Frisco."

"Huh!" his sister sniffed. "It's not the heated pool

you're missing, it's that silly girlfriend of yours who's chasing after you."

Grover's handsome face turned a fiery red as he snapped, "Just keep your mouth shut about her, Sis. That's my business!"

Richard Wells had by now reached the waves coming in from deeper water and was turning his board shoreward to ready himself for the wave he wanted. Audrey watched, her eyes sparkling with the joy of being once again on a beach with the water and sky extending and encompassing her as they had back on Waimanalo Beach. A wave rose behind the painter, but it was only a small one, and he let it pass by. As the shorebound swell lifted his board, he glanced back to look at the other waves forming. A large wave set up its momentum, and he dug in and sent his board flying, starting straight off with it, his board at right angles to it. As the swell came and the nose of the board tipped down, he agilely clambered to his feet, turning and leaning away from the breaking portion of the wave as it caught his board, then leaning further into it as it reached its steepness. White water broke over the back of the board, and spray slashed at him, but he rode the wave to its ebb, then flattened himself on the board and took the afterwash.

"That was beautiful!" Audrey exulted, turning to Beatrice. "There must be such a wonderful feeling of freedom to ride the waves all by yourself and to keep your balance. It's like flying!" The redhead shrugged indifferently. "I suppose it's fun. Right now it looks like a lot of work to me. After you're washed back to shore, you have to start all over again. There wouldn't really be much to it unless you were competing with somebody." She cast Audrey an appraising glance, the corners of her lips tightening. "I'll bet I could beat you at it, if I had a mind to."

"You probably could," Audrey cheerfully agreed. "Don't forget, I only paddled a little bit when I was a kid, and I never really did any surfing. And you're an awfully good swimmer, Bee; I'm sure you'll learn it much faster than I will."

Again the painter was taking the crest of a wave, his body bent like a skier's, poised aloft on the very tip of a high wave that sent him far in toward the shore. After its ebb, he paddled back to the rocks, leaped off, guided the board back to shallow water, and walked toward the trio. "That'll give you an idea of what it's like," he chuckled. "The trick is to figure out which is your wave. Right now, we're all alone and there's nobody else to worry about. If you ever get to a crowded beach, where there's a lot of surfers around you, then it's really tricky. But this is our own private stretch, and nobody's gonna bother us this summer. Wanna try it, kids?"

And thus began for Audrey Mason the most idyllic summer she had known since leaving Hawaii. As the painter had predicted, she learned swiftly out of what he called a natural ability. One of the beginner's greatest handicaps in surfing off a rocky coast like Santa Cruz is the fear of being "wiped out," of being knocked off a surfboard by a wave or by another surfer. But Audrey did not have this fear because her confidence had come when she was a child with Milliama. And too, expert swimmer that she was, she knew that even if she were knocked off the surfboard by a towering wave or one that fell too short after its crest, she was in no danger. Within a week, she had learned to wax the board Richard Wells had lent her, to paddle out, her muscles relaxed and her strength conserved for the tension of entering the waves lashing forward, then to poise herself aloft on the board with left foot forward and body bent at the angle that gave her full control.

Rather piqued by her cousin's display of rudimentary skill, Beatrice practiced assiduously to keep pace with Audrey. As for Grover, he found this unspoken rivalry amusing, and it served to distract him from his involvement with Jessica Laswell. Though not the swimmer that his sister and Audrey were, he went out with them and

67

tried to match their growing proficiency. Richard Wells encouraged this, because the really good surfer must have the test of surfing with others near him, so as to learn how to shift his body to turn the board when collision with another surfer seems imminent, and to develop that coordination which brings confidence and the fullest enjoyment from the exciting sport. It was usually Grover who was "wiped out," tumbling off his board and diving under a large wave while his board skimmed on through the "soup" of crashing white water that follows after the breaking of a wave. And then it was that Audrey and Beatrice had to call upon their utmost agility to avoid the danger of the heavy riderless board.

The painter showed them many of the safety rules of good surfing, a sport with its own code of ethics in which consideration for others plays a vital part. He showed them how to judge a set of waves to determine which individual crest should be ridden, how to take the wave at right angles and to exult in the sense of motion when the nose of the board tips down, the tail rises, and the surfer begins to slide with the wave, capturing the energy of sea and surf and mastering it. Once having caught the wave, the surfer must turn and lean away from the breaking portion, and here the sensation becomes akin to flying. Instinctively, at the steepest part of the wave, the surfer goes to his knees and leans farther into the wave, white water breaking over the back of the board and spray lashing at his eyes. Wells showed them how one can ride straight off the break into the white water and keep the nose of the surfboard up to prevent pearling, which would throw the body off-balance. Another vital safety precaution was learning to turn turtle, gripping the board tightly and rolling over when, in paddling out, the surfer is met by a heavy wave that breaks in front of him.

Margery Mason found it a relief to be left to her own devices with Sue Wells, seeing that her "little brood," as she referred to the trio, had found themselves a new interest. She and Sue made many visits to Carmel to visit several of Sue's artist friends, for Margery Mason considered herself an avowed patroness of the arts and told Sue that she might find some brilliant new paintings or ceramics or sculpture or even hand-made jewelry for Dan's shop. She had occasionally backed her own judgment and invested some of his money in such "artistic creations," and invariably they had been commercial fiascos. However, she had always remained undaunted by his dour criticism; and by the time it was time to head back for San Francisco, she had spent several hundred dollars on artifacts that were doomed to gather dust on the back shelves of the store on O'Farrell Street.

Beatrice and Grover Mason were, when all is said and done, eager to get back to San Francisco and paid Richard and Sue Wells only perfunctory thanks for their hospitality. But Audrey, who had enjoyed two magical months of the freedom and exhilaration she had not known since she had been a child, gratefully expressed her appreciation for the kindness the couple had shown her. Richard Wells patted her on the shoulder and nodded with a smile. "It was a pleasure to have you, Audrey, a real pleasure. I guess maybe I saw a lot more of you than Sue did, but I can tell you that we both like you a lot. I don't know what you're going to be aiming at in later life, though it's my suggestion that you think about trying out for the Olympics. No, I mean it"—as Audrey started to shake her head and self-consciously blush—"you've shown some wonderful ability out there on the waves, and you were a fine swimmer to start with. Who knows, maybe someday you can try out for the championship meets at Makaha or Malibu. Anyway, good luck to you, Audrey."

"Makaha," Audrey musingly repeated. "Mother used to tell me about how the greatest swimmers, like Duke Kahanamoku, rode the waves there. He's almost a legend in Hawaii today, you know."

"Well, maybe you'll go back there someday and ride those big waves yourself, Audrey," Richard Wells assured her. "Meantime, take good care of yourself, and I hope you'll pay us a visit again next summer."

Margery Mason, at the wheel of the big sedan, blew the horn impatiently. Grover and Beatrice scowled. "It's just like her to show off by apple polishing, Grover," the redhead muttered to her brother. "Mother and we already said thanks to them for having us come down here, but no, Audrey has to go and make a production of it. No wonder she's been a teacher's pet all the way back from grade-school days. Sometimes she gets me so mad!"

Audrey Mason shook hands with Sue and Richard Wells again and then turned toward the car. Her eyes were shining, and there was a beauty to her face that was strangely akin to that of her dead mother. It was the same serene and guileless beauty Philip Mason himself had discovered, a beauty that was to end his wandering and decide his own destiny. A destiny that was to be fulfilled by the daughter he had known only as a tiny baby. And even he could not have dreamed what her destiny was to be.

Chapter
EIGHT

IN THE FALL, Beatrice and Audrey entered junior classes at San Francisco University, while Grover commenced his senior year. Dan Mason's business experienced a somewhat comforting upsurge, thanks in part to several large conventions that brought tourists from the East Coast swarming along O'Farrell Street. Indeed, business was so good that he wryly commented to Margery, "For a change, a couple of the things you picked up in Carmel this summer actually sold. Wonders will never cease!"

Dan Mason's pleasure in this mild advent of prosperity after several lean seasons was further enhanced by his pride in Grover's athletic accomplishments. The football team had elected Grover captain, and Dan took Margery and the girls to Kezar Stadium to see the opening game against College of the Pacific. Grover's team was a four-touchdown favorite, and from the opening gun it was apparent that the sportswriters had called the exact turn on the contest. In the first half, Grover caught an opponent's fumble and ran through a broken field some sixty yards for the first score. Before the half had ended, he had scored another touchdown as a pass receiver and contributed to the scoring of a third with his own accurately placed pass to the star left end. Dan Mason basked in the cheers around him, and though he prided himself on being sophisticated and shrewd in his business dealings, he could not refrain from looking around at the cheering spectators and saying with an air of casual commentary, "That's my son who just scored the touchdown."

The game ended in a romp for San Francisco University by the score of forty-one to six, and Grover himself scored a total of four touchdowns and kicked two conversions. It was a day of glory for Dan Mason, so much so that he not only took his wife, daughter, and Audrey out to Grison's Steak House for a celebration dinner, but also insisted that Grover's football coach accompany them all.

"Great game today, Mr. Maitland," Dan Mason exulted. "Waiter, pour Mr. Maitland some more wine. And some for my son, too. I guess it's all right, Coach, if the star of the team has one glass of wine after a big game like today's, eh?" he chuckled, beaming expansively at everyone around the private table at the rear that he had commandeered.

Grover flushed and squirmed uncomfortably in his seat. "Cut it down, Dad," he mumbled, furtively glancing at Coach Maitland, a sturdy, nearly bald man in his early fifties. "There were ten other guys out there on the field besides me, Dad."

"Now, now, Grover, no need to be modest, not in the bosom of your family. Isn't that right, Coach?" Dan Mason refused to be rebuffed on so joyous an occasion. "I'm glad you accepted my invitation, Coach. I want to talk to you about Grover's future. D'you think he might make All-American? It'd be wonderful his senior year."

"Oh, for God's sake, Dad," Grover protested, trying to efface himself, his face scarlet now with embarrassment. Audrey gave him a sympathetic look. He had never really accepted her as a member of the family, but he at least had shown her the respect of one equal to another. Part of that, she rightly guessed, could be attributed to the skill she had shown at swimming and surfing this past summer. Grover had told her the last day that she was "pretty darn good for a girl," and that was the highest praise of which he was capable. She felt sorry to see him made the cynosure by his own father in front of a comparative stranger. Whatever else Grover's faults might be, he was a very competent athlete and was certain to have a keen sense of pride. To point him out and ask for an appraisal in this way was humiliating, even if his father meant it to display his affection for Grover.

Donald Maitland scratched his chin, shot a look that was half amusement, half irritation at Dan Mason, and guardedly replied, "No reason why a player shouldn't aim high, Mr. Mason. You've got to have ambition in any game to be outstanding, if you can back it up with ability. And Grover's a pretty fair scatback in my book. Let's wait till we get to some of the tougher games in the schedule."

But even this wary riposte did not dampen Dan Mason's enthusiasm. "Well, of course, Coach," he chuckled, "I've really got you at a disadvantage off in a corner like this. And I know you can't be expected to show favoritism, just because Grover happens to be my son. But you've got to admit he looked great out there this afternoon. I'm hoping for big things from Grover."

"I'm sure you are, Mr. Mason," was the bland reply. "And I'd hate to see you disappointed. Guess that leaves it up to you, Grover. And the best way to prove anything is out there on the field against the other teams. Right?"

"Sure, Coach." Grover, clearly unhappy to be the target of this dialogue, went back to his steak with the guarded concentration of one who wants to be left in peace.

Later that evening, after they had driven Coach Maitland back to his attractive duplex apartment on Twin Peaks, Dan Mason continued to extol his son's athletic prowess till at last Beatrice tartly exclaimed, "For heaven's sake, Dad, you'll wind up giving Grover a swelled head, if he doesn't already have one!"

And at last the importer allowed the topic to subside. Grover, in the back seat of the family Buick, turned to his right to glance at Audrey, who gave him a quick smile

73

and sympathetic nod to show that she understood his irritation. "Yeah," he muttered, "I'd just better live up to all that or I'll never hear the last of it."

After the first week in December, when Grover's team closed the season with a tie against its traditional rival, Santa Clara, it was apparent that Grover Mason was not destined to make All-American, despite his father's campaigning. The chief reason for this was the towheaded senior's deepening involvement with Jessica Laswell. During the football season, when Grover had had to keep training, he had been able to avoid frequent dates with the ambitious young woman, but now he no longer had an excuse. And with the holidays ahead, Jessica firmly intended to be squired wherever she could be seen in the company of the handsome young football star of San Francisco University.

Audrey decided that teaching was the career she wished to follow after her formal studies. One of her friends at the university was an education major, a twenty-one-year-old, gregarious brown-haired girl named Sylvia Mordaunt. They had shared a table one afternoon at the campus malt shop, and Sylvia had recognized Audrey as the brilliant young swimmer whose picture, as a possible Olympic star, had been published in the San Francisco *Chronicle*. She had introduced herself, and they had begun to talk about classes and professors, and finally Sylvia had gone on to explain why she wanted so very much to be a teacher. Her parents had come from the East and had both died in an automobile accident when she was only twelve, she explained. A wealthy spinster aunt had become her guardian, and Sylvia had felt so constrained and so much of a stranger in her aunt's gloomy house on Buchanan Street where she lived that she had determined to fit herself for a role in which she might work with impressionable and eager youngsters to whom she could impart her own previously thwarted zest for life and the acquisition of practical knowledge by which to meet its many challenges.

Audrey had felt a warm bond of fellowship for Sylvia,

because her own life had much in common with the older girl's. She, like Sylvia, was an orphan, and in spite of the apparent friendliness and cordiality both Daniel and Margery Mason showed her, she had never ceased to regard herself an alien who did not belong in their house and who was permitted to live there only out of charity. The thought of earning her own way had often occurred to her; indeed, she was extremely conscious that her tuition to the university had been paid for by Dan Mason. She had heard him complain about failing business so many times that she was made all the more acutely aware of exactly what her upbringing and schooling were costing him.

And finally, there was the memory of her mother. The memory of what Milliama had told her about her father and how he had come from Chicago because his health was bad and because he wanted to seek restoration of body and soul amid the serene beauty and peace of Oahu. And yet he had gone back to teaching school and had taken greater joy from it than in his previous work on the mainland, because he had been so impressed by the lesson of brotherhood and the mixing of races he could observe every day in his classroom. Milliama had explained it so simply and so beautifully that Audrey had never forgotten her mother's words. "Your father, Aukele, was like a man who has been born again. It is as if he was sent to this island with *aloha* already in his heart so that he could see how everyone lives together happily, and so that he could teach the new children each year this wonderful lesson."

If she became a teacher, Audrey reasoned, she could earn her own livelihood and be accountable only to herself; perhaps she could even repay Dan Mason for the cost of her education.

But a week after Grover Mason's graduation in June, Audrey's growing inclination toward her father's own profession was diverted in a way that she herself would never have desired.

Throughout the spring, determined Jessica Laswell

75

had renewed her efforts to hold Grover to the casual promise of marriage he had made to her the previous summer. The wonder was that she did not realize it for what it really was—an understandably masculine way of being devious so as to prolong the very desirable relationship she had accorded him. Moreover, it was Grover's first essay into carnal love, and he found it so fascinating an experience and Jessica so rewardingly complaisant that he had no wish to end a good thing. The year before, it had been easy enough to put Jessica off by telling her that once he had finished school, they could be married. And then the intensive training of the football season had separated them, only to leave him with an intense desire to renew their intimacy by the time of the Christmas holidays. The liaison continued more or less irregularly until the fateful week after Grover's graduation.

In the main, his father was well satisfied with Grover's accomplishments. He had finished with a commendable B-minus scholastic average, and though he had not been named as one of the finest football players in the country, he had nevertheless managed to be cited by several of the California sportswriters as a candidate for all-state honors, and some had even ranked him as an alternate on the hypothetical third team of all-American. As a reward, Dan Mason took Grover's car to a dealer with whom he had previously done business and whose wife was a frequent customer of his own shop and traded it in for a dazzling new white Thunderbird convertible. If it cost him a little more than he really wanted to spend at the time, because business had begun to slacken in June when San Franciscans started to take their vacations, he told himself that Grover had more than earned it.

And on a Friday evening, exactly three days after his father had presented him with the Thunderbird, Grover Mason left the old house on Lombard Street after supper, saying that he had a date with an assistant coach of the 49'ers, the celebrated professional team that represented the city of San Francisco. There was a chance, he told his father, that he might be offered a trial with the team. Dan and Margery Mason had planned to go to the Curran on Geary and Taylor to see the inimitable Gwen Verdon in *Damn Yankees* and had expected Grover to accompany them with Beatrice and Audrey. But the tempting prospect of having his son a professional football star overrode Dan Mason's momentary annoyance at having his plans altered, and he urged Grover, "Be sure you don't sell yourself short, boy. If they're interested in you, they'll be willing to pay a bonus for signing. Maybe I ought to go along with you just to make sure they offer you a good contract. I'm a pretty shrewd businessman, you know, Grover boy." But Grover evaded his father's offer by saying that this was just a preliminary talk and that of course he would let his father meet with the assistant coach when the talk got down to the serious stage. He hurried over to his mother and kissed her, his handsome face taut with impatience. A moment later, the front door of the old house slammed behind him, and Dan Mason chuckled as he heard the Thunderbird's engine roar into life and then fade away into the distance. "I wish I had half his energy, Margery honey," he sighed. "But I guess it's enough for me to sit back and be proud that he's going to carry on the Mason name. Maybe he'll do so well that I'll have to put off his taking over the store, Margery, who knows?"

Grover Mason was not destined to take over his father's store nor to star at Kezar Stadium as a professional football player. The telephone was ringing when Beatrice, Audrey, Dan Mason, and his wife entered the house after the show. It was a little after midnight. When Dan Mason strode to the phone and picked it up, his face went ashen and he swayed like a tree bending to a sudden gale. He had just been informed that Grover Mason and a girl, not yet identified, had been found dead in the wreckage of a white Thunderbird convertible near Muir Woods.

Jessica Laswell's determination to marry Grover Mason

had cost both of them their lives. He had driven her out to Sausalito, where they had stopped to have a few drinks, and then on up the winding, narrow dirt road that led into Muir Woods, where they had parked and made love. And then Jessica Laswell had demanded that he fulfill his promise of marriage, since there could be no further obstacle to it now. Grover Mason had hedged and tried to put her off again, saying that he had to get a job first and make a living for them both, whereupon Jessica had hysterically accused him of having wanted to put her off all along and fiercely insisted that he drive her back home. As they started back down the road, she had suddenly wrenched the steering wheel away from him, and the car had plunged off the road into a ravine several hundred feet below. They had both been killed instantly. There would be no heir to carry on Dan Mason's name nor to inherit the import shop on O'Farrell Street.

Chapter
NINE

THIRTEEN YEARS AGO, when she had first entered the house on Lombard Street on that rainy November evening, Audrey Mason had sensed, child though she was, an isolation and a brooding atmosphere about and within it. Though it was summer now, and San Francisco was at its loveliest, the house now seemed enshrouded with shadows even when the sun's rays managed to fleck the steps of the wide veranda. There were shadows of psychological mood, yet so palpable as to be real. And her discussions with Sylvia Mordaunt, which had all but decided her to work for a teacher's certificate upon graduation so that she might surround herself with the eager and the young whose very animation could banish the shadows that lurked everywhere in the old house, took on a more purposeful resolve after Grover's death.

And yet the bitter knowledge that she was still dependent upon Dan Mason's indulgence and charity harassed her with each new day after the tragic accident. Dan Mason had aged overnight. At first he had refused to believe that it was his son whom the police had found in the wrecked car. "My boy doesn't run around with girls," he had told the traffic officer who had come to the house immediately after that fateful phone call which had left him dazed, horrified, and incredulous. But the identification had been plain; Grover's wallet and fraternity key and the license of the car defied Dan Mason's unwillingness to believe that the hope of his life had suddenly, uselessly been snuffed out. The next day, Jessica's mother, vituperative in her vengeful grief, had phoned him, and then he had found out about the subterfuges his supposedly trustworthy and ethical son had used during the past year to continue a clandestine liaison that would never have had his official sanction. Jessica's mother had told him that her daughter had confided in her how Grover had promised to marry her after he had finished his schooling. Nothing came of her threats, nothing except the tormenting grief that burned like vitriol and would not be allayed.

"If only he'd told me about that girl," Dan would keep saying to Margery Mason during those first dreadful weeks which followed the quiet funeral. "He knew I would have given him everything I had. I could have advised him if he'd only come to me. I always gave him everything he wanted. Why didn't he tell me about Jessica? I'd have straightened things out. She wasn't worthy of my son, you know that as well as I do. He had a great future ahead of him, and now there's nothing left. Nothing."

Sue and Richard Wells had already extended an invitation to the Masons to spend the summer with them again at Santa Cruz. That was out of the question, of course. Audrey felt more and more like a stranger each time she sat down at the dinner table. Beatrice was melancholy too, and Margery Mason gave up her whirlwind round of social activity, preferring to sit in the living room opposite her husband, silently reading. She too showed the ravages of grief, and often late at night Audrey, whose room was next to hers, could hear her weeping for her dead son.

So as the summer dragged on through August, Audrey felt herself a prisoner as well as an interloper who had against her will been forced to become a helpless and ignored participant to a tragedy. For Grover's death seemed to have brought about a subtle deterioration. It was intangible, yet real. Audrey shared their meals, even at times their conversations, and yet she sensed herself as a spectator who looked through a partly opaque glass through which she could observe the actions of those who are kept apart from her. That barrier became almost unendurable, for sensitive as she was by nature, she had no wish to intrude upon their grief or to remind Dan Mason that she still lived in his house and accepted his bounty while his sturdy young son, the hope of his twilight years, was gone forever.

More than ever, Audrey wanted to go on for her senior year at San Francisco University. But now there was the constantly intensifying awareness that, since she was not yet of age by California law—it would be another year before she was twenty-one and granted the independence of an adult—Dan Mason would have to stand the cost of this final term. Seeing how drawn and haggard his face had become, his eyes lusterless and brooding, sitting reading a book or a newspaper in the evening in his favorite armchair and sometimes lifting his head and looking off into space for long moments, she felt that it would be tactless to ask for herself, who had only the status of a blood relation, what Beatrice could claim as her rightful due.

Not wanting to stay in the living room with the three of them and inwardly agonize with them through these painful silences, she often went up again to the dormer where she had spent so much time as a child, pretending that it was the little tower back on Waimanalo Beach. As the time neared for enrollment at the university, Audrey decided at last upon a course of action that would justify her continued presence in this old house where unexpected death had suddenly stopped the normal unfolding of a family's hopes and dreams. All these years, she had remembered from that last day on the beach what Luke had told her. If what Luka had said was true, then she was not improvident but an heiress of possession, possession she could barter, if need be, for her keep. Yet the thought of parting with that house on the beach on the island where she had been born would be a denial

81

of her own parents, who had loved her. No, there must be another way. And yet, since she was only a year away from the time when whatever possessions her parents had left her would be turned over to her, it was time she spoke about the matter to Uncle Dan.

It was the evening of Labor Day, and Beatrice and Margery had gone out to dinner and the theater. Dan Mason had told them that he wanted to look over the ledgers of the shop and that an outing would do them both good. He was in the library, just off the dining room, seated at an old cherrywood secretary, and he was studying the accounts when Audrey hesitantly entered.

"I didn't mean to disturb you, Uncle Dan," she said.

He laid down the pencil he had been using to check the columns of figures and turned in his chair to face her at the doorway. Audrey was appalled at the dull, unseeing look in his eyes, which seemed to have hollowed in their sockets, at his flaccid cheeks and jowls, and at the nervous twitching of his mouth. There were deep lines in his forehead, and he reached now into his lapel pocket for a pair of reading glasses. "Perfectly all right, Audrey. Come in, my dear. Matter of fact, I'm glad you did. I guess I've been straining my eyes over the books, and I forgot my glasses. Sit down." He gestured to a heavy straight-backed chair with thick plush seat.

"Thank you. Uncle Dan, I've been wanting to talk to you about—about staying on here."

He adjusted his glasses, frowned, massaged the back of his neck as if the muscles ached, then turned back to the desk and closed the ledger. Then he rose from the chair, walked over to a deep armchair opposite her, and seated himself. "Staying on here, Audrey? I don't quite understand."

She flushed and lowered her eyes. "I've been very grateful to you and Aunt Margery for all you've done for me since Mother died. But I know how terrible it's been for both of you ever since . . ." She let the words trail off, watching him nod, then close his eyes for a moment. "If it hadn't happened, I'd probably have gone on to school this fall and finished my last year. You see, I think I want to be a teacher, the way my father was. But now, Uncle Dan, I don't feel I have a right to ask you to go on paying for my education. I know that things haven't been too good at the shop, because I've heard you say so."

"I'm not exactly a pauper yet," he retorted with a flash of his old decisiveness. "You're very thoughtful, Audrey. You've been like a daughter to us, and we've tried to make you happy here."

"I know you have, Uncle Dan," she said softly, "but I think it's time I took a job and earned my keep. I'd feel better about it, really I would. I can take night courses, or maybe when things are better later on, I can go back and get my degree. But there's something else."

His eyes widened questioningly as he stared at her, waiting for her to go on.

"My father and mother had that house on the beach in Oahu, Uncle Dan. Luka—she was Mother's sister, you remember—told me that it would be mine someday. You're my guardian till I'm twenty-one, and that will be a year from next month. But I wanted to ask you about it. Maybe, if things aren't going well for you, I could sell it and give you the money to pay you back for all you've done for me."

"Of course not, my dear. I'd be a fine guardian, I would, to think of having you do a thing like that. Your father was very close to me, Audrey, and I guess in a way I was really the one who sent him on to Hawaii. When his health was bad after he left Chicago and he came here to visit, I told him that a vacation on the islands would be just what the doctor ordered. Well, he stayed there and made a life of it, and now you're all that's left. But I'll admit that your taking a job might not be such a bad idea. You can't be sure that there'll be a place for you as a teacher, and that's more than a year away, anyhow. If you do go to work in a good office, you can have money of your own, and maybe you'll even prefer a business career to teaching."

"I'm going to look for a job next week, Uncle Dan. But I still want to repay you if I can."

He shook his head. "I wouldn't hear of such a thing, Audrey. However, I'm glad you reminded me about that house on the beach there. I think it would be a good idea for me to visit Honolulu—I've been meaning to take a trip there for quite a long time, to bring back things that might sell well in my shop. And I could check the legal title of the house and the land. That will have to be done next year anyway when you come of age."

"But Luka—" she began, and then an inexplicable impulse made her halt the sentence. How long ago it had been . . . what had Luka said to her that last day on the beach? Something about her keeping the secret and that she must tell no one, because it was her own inheritance, and no one else must have it.

"What were you going to say about Luka, my dear?"

"I—nothing really, Uncle Dan. It's been so long ago. She hasn't written to us now for nearly a year, has she?"

"No, that's true, Audrey. The first year you were here with us, I remember that she wrote at least once a month. I daresay she knows that you're settled and happy. You showed me her last letter, which came just before last Christmas, you remember."

"Yes. Poor Luka still doesn't have any children of her own. Maybe that was why she was so wonderful to me and looked after me when Mother had to go away in the evenings to work."

Dan Mason rose from the chair and walked over to Audrey. He put his hand on her shoulder and looked down at her with as benign a smile as he could muster. "If you like, my dear, I'll try to help you find a job. You're a very bright young woman, and it shouldn't be too difficult. Come to think of it, the broker who handles my insurance and the coverage for the shop might just need someone in his office."

"That's very good of you, Uncle Dan."

"Not really." He gave a forced little laugh. "But if you really want to go on to the university this fall, Audrey, things aren't so bad that I couldn't manage your tuition and expenses."

"No." She shook her head as she stared levelly at him. "I don't want to ask for anything more, Uncle Dan. Getting out into the world wouldn't be a bad idea for me anyway. A person really can't be a good teacher unless she knows what it's really like outside the classroom too. Anyway, I'd feel a lot better earning money of my own."

"I told you you're like my own daughter, Audrey dear. And I'm going to take you up on that notion about going to Honolulu and looking up the records on your parents' property. As your guardian, I owe you an accounting. Besides, I don't think it would do me any harm to have a little vacation too."

He walked with her toward the door, an arm around her shoulders. He looked very tired, very old, very lost. She felt tears well to her eyes. "I know how much you miss him, Uncle Dan," she whispered. "I can't tell you how sorry I feel."

"Thank you, my dear. You've been a comfort. Yes, there are times when I wonder why I keep going on with the shop, killing myself to make a small profit when business conditions keep getting worse. It was all for him and Beatrice. Now there's just Beatrice. And she'll get married someday, and there won't be any one to carry on my name."

There was nothing she could say to assuage the anguished remembrance of his son. Never before in all her life had she felt so utterly a stranger, so completely an intruder. He had listened to her, he had replied to her, and yet it had been as if she had not been present in the room at all. Each time he looked at her, she felt sure, he was remembering Grover living here, growing to manhood, on the threshold of achieving all the fine plans Dan Mason had evolved for him. She would not have blamed Dan Mason very much if he had openly told her that he resented her being here now that Grover had been taken from him. That was why she must find her own independence and her own solution. Without them, her life, too, might well become forfeit to the gloomy shadows that pervaded the old house on Lombard Street.

Chapter
TEN

EVEN THOUGH he was still despondent over Grover's loss, Dan Mason found his visit to Honolulu a complete revelation. It had been thirteen years since the China Clipper had landed him at the modest-sized airport on his journey to bring back the child of his dead cousin. Now the International Airport was really imposing, and after he had gone down the ramp from the big Pan American plane, a pretty brown-skinned girl in traditional Hawaiian costume had come up to him, placed a lei of white and pale yellow ginger about his neck, and kissed him on the cheek. Taken by surprise, he had relaxed his dour expression for a moment and actually flushed.

The time before, there had been only three hotels on Waikiki Beach. The pink stucco edifice of the lordly Royal Hawaiian, with its eighteen acres of landscaped park, still dominated the famous beach, but there were others to rival its splendor for the tourists. He had made reservations at the new Reef, which stood beside the Halekulani, and when the friendly bellboy carried his suitcase into the spacious and attractive lobby, he realized at a glance that Hawaii was no longer just a territory or an isolated spot on the globe for the itinerant traveler. There were crowds of tourists here, young and old alike, and the bustle and hum of conversation reminded him of the opening morning of a convention at the St. Francis or the Mark Hopkins back in San Francisco. The recognition of statehood had focused the spotlight of tourist interest on this glamorous tropical retreat.

Hitherto, Dan Mason had imported palm-tree-seed and shell necklaces and many other decorative trinkets for his own tourist trade by sending his elderly yet shrewdly capable chief clerk, Fred Perry. Perry was nearly sixty now, but even a generation ago he had been the same fastidious and circumspect man that he was today. He had lived with an old-maid sister most of his life, his hobbies were hiking and reading, and he despised night-clubs and immodestly dressed women. On the other hand, he could drive as hard a bargain in buying lots of merchandise for the shop as Dan himself, and so in the past Dan had entrusted the annual trips to Honolulu to him, preferring to stay home and do his best to improve slow business. Now, quite suddenly, he felt exhilarated after this thirteen-year absence, and he was very glad that he had come.

It was a mere five-hour journey from San Francisco on the Pan-Am plane he had just left, and it had been infinitely more comfortable than the China Clipper that had carried him to Honolulu thirteen years ago. It was six in the evening, and there was still no hint of dusk, but there was little more that he could do now except to go up to his room and change for dinner, then stroll along the main thoroughfare and see the shops. In the morning, he would visit the Bureau of Conveyances. He had no doubt that everything was in order. He had sent a check for taxes on Philip Mason's property with unfailing regularity every year, so there was no danger that the land and the house had been forfeited. And then he would visit Luka and tell her that Audrey was fine, and after that he would do a little shopping to see what might go well on O'Farrell Street.

He went upstairs in the elevator with the bellboy, and he was thinking that before that last visit thirteen years ago, he had been to Honolulu just twice. The first time had been on his honeymoon with Margery, and they had stayed at the Royal Hawaiian. The second time had been two years later, when Fred Perry had been taken ill with pneumonia and he himself had had to make the buying trip. He had thought about staying at the Royal Hawaiian this time, but it had painful memories for him . . . they had stayed a month, more than he could really afford, but Margery had been so happy there. Very likely Grover had been conceived on that honeymoon, and now Grover was dead. He did not think that he would even go into the magnificent park that fringed that lavish pink building. That part of his life was gone, and to think about it hurt too much.

He showered, changed clothes, and then had a cab take him down Kalakaua Avenue all the way out to Diamond Head, that identifying landmark of Waikiki Beach known the world over. It was, he knew, an extinct volcano, and legend had it that it once had been the home of the awesome fire goddess Pele herself. The beam of the lighthouse sent its long, luminous, pointing finger far out to sea; and as he got out of the cab he caught the sight of tiny red and green lights in the dark sky near the beam, the lights of planes winging to the neighboring islands, like Maui and the big island Hawaii itself.

He paid the driver and dismissed him, wanting to walk back to the Queen's Surf and enjoy the famous buffet dinner and then the spectacular dancing, later have a drink at the Barefoot Bar and hear the music of Sterling Mossman and his fine band, which some of his customers had recommended as being as good as the big-name group playing nightly in the Fairmont.

He had read the ads about Honolulu in the *Chronicle* and the *Examiner*, and there was no doubt that this newest state was energetically developing revenue by attracting ever-increasing numbers of visitors. It was certainly a vacation paradise, practically the year round. Indeed, if he had sufficient capital, he would think very seriously of investing it right here in Honolulu. Anyone who owned property along Waikiki Beach or any of the nearby beaches was certain to be well off in the future.

It was a pity that he hadn't thought about such an investment for his own family a good many years ago.

He fumbled in his shirt pocket for a crumpled pack of cigarettes, lit one, and stood looking out at the ocean. The blueness of the water was black now, and yet it stretched endlessly until, if you looked with all your might, you could see it join the lowering curve of the sky far in the distance. The air was warm but not unpleasantly so, and the smell of the ocean and of the palm trees was a heady wine. And the cloying sweetness of that ginger lei that girl had put about his neck seemed somehow to blend. He stood lost in reverie until the heat of the burning cigarette made him grimace and look down at his hand. He crushed the cigarette underfoot and turned back along Kalakaua Avenue toward the Queen's Surf. . . .

It had been more than usually crowded at the popular buffet this evening, and a few minutes after he had sat down at a table for two with his heavily laden tray of roast beef, salad, slices of sweet fresh pineapple, and yams, a bespectacled little man, looking helplessly about for a place to sit, asked, "Would you mind if I shared your table?"

At first Dan Mason had wanted to say that he did mind very much, and yet somehow, tonight, remembering the first terrible weeks that had followed Grover's death, he suddenly wanted to talk to someone, to feel himself a part of the gay camaraderie that characterized this place. It was a handsome old house, and where the buffet was, facing the ocean, you could look right out at the beach and the water beyond. There was a palm grove all around. And just beyond the buffet, in a kind of garden, there were rows of tables and chairs around a platform where three times a night the talented dancers put on a show and even went down to the audience to bring up some of the male guests to dance with them. It was quite a place, Dan Mason thought enviously. They must use at least fifty rounds of beef a night. And they probably took in more in one night than his shop did in two whole weeks.

"Sure, go ahead," he heard himself saying. "Glad to have company. My name's Dan Mason."

The little man, he saw, was probably a Filipino, with thinning black hair and an enormous forehead and quickly darting black eyes behind horn-rimmed spectacles. He beamed at Dan Mason, bobbed his head in embarrassment as he quickly emptied his tray and set it to one side atop Dan's, then seated himself, drew out his wallet, and with a flourish presented an engraved card.

"My name is Estaban Aguinaldo, Mr. Mason, at your service," he said pleasantly. "I take it you're a *malihini*?"

"I guess, from the way I'm looking around and taking all this in, you'd probably guess this was my first trip, señor Aguinaldo," Dan Mason cheerfully replied. He was pleasantly surprised to find that the surroundings and this unexpected sharing of a table had brightened the gloomy mood that had followed him from the very moment he had set foot on the plane in San Francisco. "Actually, it's about my third trip. I was here first at the Royal Hawaiian on my honeymoon. I have an import shop back in San Francisco." He glanced idly at the card his unctuous companion had just handed him. It read, "Estaban Aguinaldo, Real Estate, 269½ Lewers Road, Phone 331-96." He looked at his companion with greater interest as he pocketed the card. "So you're in real estate? I imagine you're doing a booming business."

The little Filipino began to slice his roast beef into convenient bites before beginning his meal. He chuckled and nodded. "That is an understatement, señor Mason. This year of nineteen sixty has been a remarkable one for Hawaii. There is probably more wealth being widely shared than ever before in the history of the islands."

"I could see when I checked into the Reef earlier this evening how many hotels have been built along the beach," Dan Mason agreed.

91

"That is only part of it, señor Mason. Last year, the new state government owned thirty-two percent of all the land in Hawaii, the federal government nearly eight percent. Twelve of the big private landowners still own thirty percent, and the Hawaiian Homes Commission has two and a half percent. The small-property owners, like an individual person, señor, own only about twenty-seven percent of the land. The development of education as well as building and commercial enterprises like these hotels you have seen are bringing people here as never before. Once it was said that pineapple and sugarcane brought the money to Hawaii. Now and in the future it will be the tourists. Yes, business is very good for me, señor Mason."

"I've read a little bit about the history of Hawaii, of course," Dan Mason asserted as he forked a mouthful of salad. "But isn't most of the commercial business centered right around Waikiki Beach?"

The little Filipino shook his head. "Not at all, señor Mason. Oh, it is true enough that thus far most of the building has been here on Oahu, and the other islands are as yet undiscovered so far as the tourists are concerned. But that will change, too, someday soon. There are many developments on leased land taking place where there used to be ranches or farms or even on land that had no improvement at all and was considered worthless. The population is increasing, too, and that is good for the real estate business also. Do you know perhaps that Oahu acquired more than a hundred thousand new residents in the five years just before statehood? And the biggest jump in population has been in the Kailua-Kaneohe-Waimanalo area, practically double."

"Waimanalo," Dan Mason thoughtfully repeated. "Then land along Waimanalo Beach should have some value?"

The Filipino took a swallow of iced tea to wash down a bite of the succulent roast beef. "There is no doubt of it, señor Mason. Windward Oahu is no longer considered country land. Those who work in Honolulu during the day and drive back to the homes they have had built on leased land in the region I have just mentioned now use four-lane highways and two big tunnels. The famous Pali pass has been tunneled out for the modern automobile. And all of this population increase has meant much more retail trade and the shipping in of goods. Oh, we are developing our industries slowly, señor Mason, but the principal business is going to be tourists."

"I have a friend," Dan Mason guardedly ventured, "who owns an acre of land on Waimanalo Beach, with a fine house and garden. He is wondering if he should sell it now or wait."

"I could of course sell it for him now, señor Mason. But if I myself owned that land—you understand that I am speaking in general terms—I should hold it for a few more years. It is my prediction that there will be tall residential buildings, perhaps hotels, perhaps apartments each of which is privately owned. This is certain to come as the tourist business grows and as many of the *haoles* decide to settle down in Oahu for good."

"How much do you think property like that would be worth today, señor Aguinaldo?"

"Well, señor Mason, as I said, it would be wise to wait a few years to get the very best price. And Waimanalo Beach is not yet Waikiki Beach, to be sure. Still, to give you an illustration, property along Kalakaua Avenue, where we are now, has been selling at prices as high as thirty to sixty dollars a square foot. Before the war, I have no doubt that it could have been purchased for a few dollars per square foot. Believe me, señor Mason, those who own land in Oahu today are in the driver's seat."

"You're quite an expert." Dan Mason smiled. "Are you going to stay for the show?"

"Yes, indeed. This is my week of vacation from my business, and I want to behave just like a *malihini*," the little Filipino replied with a broad wink. "Does this friend of yours have a real estate broker to act for him here in Honolulu?"

"No, he doesn't. The fact is that he died at the outbreak of the war, and I have been paying the taxes on the house and land ever since, holding them in trust for his daughter, who is living with me in San Francisco."

"I see. She may one day be a rather wealthy young woman, then." The little Filipino took off his glasses, vigorously wiped them with a neatly folded white handkerchief from his lapel pocket, then adjusted them. "You are here to look at this property, perhaps?"

"Yes, along with business I want to do for my shop. You've been here for some years, señor Aguinaldo?"

"My father brought me from Manila when I was ten years old and put me through the best school. He had money, so I was lucky, as you can understand. Yes, I should say that I know Oahu as well as any *kamaaina*."

"Perhaps after the show you'll let me buy you a drink upstairs at the Barefoot Bar," Dan Mason suggested.

"With the greatest of pleasure, señor Mason. And I should like very much to be of service to you in the event that you require assistance in disposing of this property."

"I wasn't exactly thinking of disposing of it, señor Aguinaldo." Dan Mason speculatively eyed the little Filipino. "As I told you, I'm holding it in trust for my cousin's daughter till she's of age next year."

"It will have even more value next year than it does now, believe me. But I think it is about time for the first show. We had better go out and get good seats so that we can see the lovely hula dancers, eh, señor Mason?"

It had been a thoroughly enjoyable evening, the first such he had allowed himself in far longer than he cared to remember. And surprisingly enough, it had cost much less than he had anticipated, for the little Filipino realtor had insisted on standing him drinks and then dropped him off at the Reef in the cab that took him on to his own house on Kapiolani Boulevard. Dan Mason had been quite impressed with his companion's knowledge of both the history and the real estate developments of Oahu. There was no doubt that his cousin Philip had got hold of a very valuable piece of land for practically a song,

94

and the longer it was held, the more its value would increase. Audrey would certainly not have to worry about her future, no matter what occupation she decided to select. Indeed, if she wanted to sell the land and the house now, she could certainly derive sufficient income to pay for her senior year at the university and have a good deal of money in the bank to tide her over for several years if she wanted to pursue an academic career.

The colorful entertainment, the sudden new companionship of the little realtor, the entire relaxing mood this visit had brought about left Dan Mason in such a state of pleased exhilaration that it was difficult for him to drop off to sleep. From the open window of his room on the tenth and topmost floor of the Reef, right on the ocean, he could hear the gentle murmuring of the waves stirred by the cooling tradewind. At last it acted as a soporific, but not before he had indulged himself in the fanciful speculation of what it would be like to live here, free of the business annoyances of the little shop on O'Farrell Street, reveling in the easy life of the island and comforted by the knowledge that he had property worth a fortune. After all the years that he had worked so diligently to provide for his family, he had, after all was said and done, not too much in the way of material possessions to show for all that effort. And yet here his cousin's daughter, who had grown up as a member of his own family, whose tuition and room and board he had so generously provided, would come into just such an ideal situation on the day of her twenty-first birthday.

He slept until ten o'clock the next morning, had breakfast sent up by room service, and then took a cab to the Bureau of Conveyances. It did not take long to verify Audrey Mason's inheritance. The Chinese clerk at the counter, who greeted him with a cordiality that would have put to shame practically all the city employees back in San Francisco, took very little time in finding the huge tract ledger in which Kalakai's original deed of sale and conveyance to Philip Mason were recorded. Yes, the taxes had been paid promptly and there was no outstanding bill or lien against the property. He thanked the clerk and left the office, then hailed a cab to take him to the house of Hanale and Luka Lopaku. It was, as he recalled from his visit thirteen years ago, about a mile from Philip's house. Then, on impulse, he told the driver to stop first near his cousin's house. Getting out of the cab, he made his way toward the wire fence that marked the boundary of Philip Mason's property. The road had been paved now, another sign of the changes that had taken place since he had brought Audrey to live with him on Lombard Street. Luka had written that she and her husband and at times one of their good friends continued to look after the house and the garden so that Audrey would find them just as they had been long ago when the time at last came for her to return to Oahu. Opening the little gate, he walked down the winding path. It seemed to him that the garden was even more beautiful and more profusely verdant in all its lavish array of fall colors than when he had seen it. And the house itself did not seem to have changed with the years. The roof had been reshingled, but the sturdy redwood frame still retained its natural color, and there was no sign of decay along its imposing timbers.

It was a beautiful house, and its owner was to be envied, he thought. He turned to look out at the gleaming white-sanded beach and the breathtaking blue expanse of water beyond it. In many ways, it had as much scenic splendor as Waikiki Beach itself. The day would come, certainly, when growing population and increased tourist traffic could make this beach a new and delightful haven for the vacationers.

Yet as guardian of this property until Audrey came of age next year, he should have the original document of sale in his possession. But he had never seen it, and that was strange. He had asked Luka about it when he had come to take Audrey back with him. He had suggested that perhaps she would find the paper in the same drawer of the secretary from which she had taken his letters to Philip and Milliama in order to learn his address in San

Francisco. But Luka had answered that the paper of which he spoke had not been in the secretary at all, and that was all she had told him. Of course, it wasn't really vital, not so long as the Bureau of Conveyances showed that the house and land were in Philip Mason's name. As his sole heir, Audrey would automatically inherit this property, even though Philip Mason had never made a will. The courts would award Philip Mason's daughter the house and land even against a lawsuit brought by any other relative, including himself.

Just the same, it would be a good thing to have the deed in his possession so that he could turn it over to Audrey on her twenty-first birthday and acquit himself of his executorship. Perhaps it was still in the secretary, hidden somewhere; perhaps that was why Luka had not found it. He walked up the steps of the house. The door was open, somewhat to his surprise. But when he entered the living room, his eyes widened to see Luka there and a young man with her. Luka had her back to him and was busy dusting the mantelpiece over the fireplace, whose huge stone structure segmented between both rooms so that it could be used on either side. To the left of the fireplace, there was a stone shelf on which seven or eight books were neatly posed between two exotically carved bookends made of *koa* wood. The young man, also standing with his back toward the door, had taken down one of the books and was looking at it.

"Good morning, Luka," he called, and Milliama's sister turned with a gasp of surprise. She was stouter than when he had last seen her, but her hair was still as sleekly black as when she had been a young girl, and her winsome face was nearly as youthful as he remembered.

"I did not expect you, Mr. Mason!" Luka exclaimed, and she seemed to look past him at the open door. "Have you brought Aukele?"

The young man turned from the stone bookshelf and came forward slowly. He was six feet tall, black-haired, sturdily but not heavily built, probably in his late twenties, Dan Mason guessed. His eyes were blue; yet singu-

97

larly his skin had the same creamy tan to it as Audrey's.

"No, Luka. I'm sorry. This is a business trip, and she couldn't come. She's doing very well at the university. Next year, when she comes of age, I'm sure that she'll visit you," he told the handsome Hawaiian matron.

"This is Kamaika Marshall," Luka explained. "He was a good friend of my father, Kalaiki, and like your cousin, Mr. Mason, he is a schoolteacher at Punaluu. He lives not far from here, and he has often helped me keep Aukele's house ready for her. We have a custom, Mr. Mason, that when the owner of a house has gone away for a long time, preparing the house as if he or she were to return the very next day will bring that person back all the sooner to the island."

"A very sentimental custom. Well, Mr. Marshall, I have you to thank as well as Luka for looking after things here for my cousin Audrey." Dan Mason offered his hand to the young schoolteacher, who shook it with a smile of welcome. Then, turning to Luka, the importer explained, "Audrey wishes me to tell you how sorry she was to learn of Llani's death last winter, and that she hopes that you and Hanale are very well indeed."

"She is such a wonderful girl, Mr. Mason, and she writes so beautifully. But I am afraid that she has forgotten nearly all the Hawaiian words Milliama and I taught her." Luka smiled sadly.

"But she is nearly a woman now, Luka. You must realize that. You have the picture that I sent you a few weeks ago. Next year she will be of age. That's why I'm here, you see."

"I do not quite understand, Mr. Mason."

"You remember, Luka, when I came here thirteen years ago to bring Audrey back to live with me, and I asked you about the paper which tells who owns this land and this house. And you said that you had not found it in the drawer of the secretary."

"That is true, Mr. Mason. I myself never saw such a paper. But I know that Milliama told me that Philip, your cousin, had shown her the proof that one day Au-

98

kele would own all that is here. And Kamaika Marshall and I come here often, because it is my hope that it will not be very much longer before I can see Aukele grown now, as you tell me, to womanhood. And the picture shows that she is even more beautiful than her mother, Milliama, Mr. Mason. All of us who knew her as a child miss her very much. You will bring her back to us, won't you?"

"It won't be until next year, Luka. She wishes to work now in an office and earn money so that she can lead her own life."

"But does she not yet have another year at the university?" Luka anxiously asked.

"Yes, Luka, but she has decided that it is better to go to work and to be independent. This is the modern spirit among young women on the mainland, you see," Dan Mason explained smilingly.

"I wish only the best for Aukele, and if it is her desire to work instead of completing her education, I wish it for her also," Luka agreed.

"Will you let me look in the secretary to find the paper, Luka?" Dan Mason asked. Luka turned to the handsome young man beside her, her eyes asking a silent question.

"There can be no harm, and he is her guardian," Kamaika Marshall responded.

Dan Mason frowned. He didn't relish the idea of an outsider's interference in a family matter. He'd never heard of this Kamaika Marshall before. That was an odd name, too. Judging from the fellow's complexion, he looked like a half-breed—a *kanaka*, that was the term people used to describe somebody of mixed blood out here in the Pacific.

"By all means, you may look for it, Mr. Mason," Luka said, "because I would not want anything to happen to keep Aukele from coming back to her home."

Again an unreasoning irritation seized the importer. He was about to reply sharply, to tell Luka and this stranger that if it hadn't been for him and his wife, Phil-

99

ip's daughter might have been a foundling. He had half a mind to tell her about the sacrifices he had made so that Audrey—and why did Luka persist in using that silly name for the girl?—could have as many advantages as Beatrice, yes, and as Grover, too. And then the thought of Grover and all that Grover had meant to him made him close his eyes for a moment to hide the sudden self-pitying tears. When at last he had got control of himself again, he said in as propitiating a tone as he could summon up under the circumstances, "You can be sure I'm not going to cheat Audrey. This is legal business, Luka. When she comes of age next year and since my cousin Philip didn't leave any will, a judge in a court may have to say who owns this house. So the paper will prove that Audrey is the rightful heir. This is why I want to look for this paper, is that clear?"

"Yes, it is clear, Mr. Mason," Luka said very calmly. "Look wherever you wish in this house. There is nothing to hide here. The door is open to welcome the daughter of your cousin and Milliama."

"Very well," Dan Mason retorted, and he could not entirely hide the pique he felt at this condescending little speech of Luka's. That was the trouble with giving these natives too much of an education, he thought, as he began to rummage through the drawer of the secretary. They fancied themselves as being people of importance. It was a good thing that he had been generous enough to bring up Philip's girl. She might have turned out to be another half-breed. At that, she was anyway. Yes, he had been very charitable all these years, and he had certainly got little credit for it. And here this native woman was telling him that she permitted him to look for a piece of paper that might make Audrey wealthier than he had ever been.

100

Chapter
ELEVEN

DAN MASON spent the rest of the afternoon and the morning of the next day visiting several of the supply centers from which Fred Perry usually procured the import items put on display in the shop on O'Farrell Street. Exquisite multicolored seashells pierced and artfully strung into necklaces, little baskets, even a few grass hula skirts for the more venturesome matrons to try out at a costume party during San Francisco's gay winter social season. Before catching the Pan-American jet that would land him at the San Francisco International Airport about seven-thirty in the evening, he telephoned Estaban Aguinaldo at the latter's office to thank the Filipino realtor once again for the pleasant evening they had shared and to ask him to keep in touch regarding any possible commercial interest in the acre on Waimanalo Beach.

"I'll be very happy to keep in contact with you, señor Mason," was the realtor's reply. "Mind you, I'm not saying that there will be any real development taking place within the next few months, but I shouldn't be surprised if within the next few years that property will be extremely valuable. After meeting you, I took the liberty —and I trust that you will pardon my presumption in the matter—of visiting the area in question. I take it that you are referring to that very handsome redwood house with the cupola and the spired weathervane?"

"That is correct, señor Aguinaldo."

"In my opinion, it is an exceptional piece of property,

Mr. Mason. The young woman for whom you are holding it in trust is extremely fortunate, I should say. It's a pity that you aren't staying here longer, because possibly you and I might discuss a way to make a very handsome profit for your ward."

"I'm going back on the flight just after lunch. But you have my address in San Francisco. If you hear of an offer for this property that you think I should know about, señor Aguinaldo, don't hesitate to write me, or even to telephone me collect."

"You have my word I shall. Again, a great pleasure for me to have met you, señor Mason. Perhaps I shall be in your beautiful city early next year. I have a brother who lives in San Diego, where he is the maître d'hôtel at one of that city's most luxurious dining rooms. He has been asking me to visit him and his wife and children, and I may do this, if my business allows me the time. Then I should be most happy to visit your shop, and perhaps you could be my guide to point out the attractions of the city. I was in San Francisco only once, and that was several years ago, and regrettably I had little time to enjoy my visit."

On the flight back to San Francisco, Dan Mason thought a good deal about his conversation with the Filipino realtor. Audrey had made him the offer of turning over the land and the house by way of fulfilling what she believed to be her obligation to him as payment for having grown up in his home. To be sure, it was a most generous offer, but it was not for a moment to be seriously considered. He would have to live with himself, and the thought that he had demanded payment for Audrey's rearing, much as if he had been the superintendent of a private orphanage, was unthinkable.

Yet when all was said and done, he had done more for her, really, than her own parents could have done, even if they had lived. After all, a schoolteacher like Philip Mason hardly made as much as he himself did in his import business and would probably not have been able to send Audrey on to the university as he had done. And then she had grown up on the mainland, as a part of a closely knit family, and surely Grover and Beatrice had been like brother and sister to her all these past years. Now she was contemplating giving up school and finding a job; well, it would not have been quite so easy in Honolulu. And he was willing to wager that even if she had found a job in Honolulu, she would have earned a great deal less than she could expect back in San Francisco. No, he had absolutely nothing for which to reproach himself in the way he had fulfilled his duty as a relative to Philip Mason. How ironic it was. If he hadn't made his suggestion to Philip to take a vacation for reasons of health out there on the islands, all this would never have happened. There would have been no child to bring up with his own family, no one on whom to spend money he might have spent on Grover or Beatrice. Grover—he thought he had been close to the boy, as close as any father to his son. God knew he had loved him and wanted only the best for him. And now all these years of self-sacrifice and money grubbing to get Grover to the top, where he belonged, were wasted, nothing to show for them. Only a headstone out at Cypress Lawn in San Mateo County to mark the fact that once a boy named Grover Mason had lived at all.

Emotion welled up in him, as bitter as gall. He took off his pince-nez, put them back in his lapel pocket, leaned back against the seat, and closed his eyes. The past seemed to swirl before him, suspended in space the way he was suspended in the big jet purring through the blue sky far above the limitless ocean. He felt a curious detachment, as if all the years had been erased and everything was beginning all over again. He was a young man again and courting Margery Gorr. He was proud of the little shop on O'Farrell Street, making plans to expand it so that he could be rich and give Margery everything she wanted. And now he was in his fifties and Margery was showing the sharp-tongued side of her nature, and she was little more than an acquaintance who had shared his house for many years, because there was not much

103

affection now between them. All he had left, really, was Beatrice, and she hadn't the slightest interest in the shop. Besides, one of these days she would be getting married, and then there would be no one at all to carry on his line or his name or to care about the shop.

The pretty blond stewardess who solicitously bent toward the stocky, gray-haired man slumped in his seat beside the window, to ask whether he would like some coffee now, was startled to see tears slowly running down his cheeks. . . .

Audrey had made up her mind. She had told Margery Mason that she definitely wasn't going back to the university this fall but instead was going to look for a job. And she wasn't going to ask for any help in finding it. In this way, she would be more on her own. "I'd like to pay for my room and board, too, Aunt Margery," she added. But Margery Mason shook her head. "No, absolutely not, Audrey. I wouldn't hear of such a thing. And neither would your Uncle Dan if he were here right now."

"But I want to lead my own life, Aunt Margery. I'm so terribly grateful for everything that you and Uncle Dan have done for me all these years. But it's not right for me to go on accepting everything from you and giving nothing in return," Audrey protested.

"I do wish you'd talk it over with your Uncle Dan when he gets back from Honolulu, dear," Margery Mason urged.

"I've already written several letters of application to ads in the newspaper, Aunt Margery. I hope I'll get an interview out of them. If I don't, I'll go down and register at some of the employment agencies. There certainly ought to be some sort of work for me, even if I don't yet have my degree," Audrey declared.

The morning after Dan Mason's return from Honolulu, there was a phone call for Audrey from Blakeley & Beale, an insurance firm on Montgomery Street, in answer to one of the letters she had sent. The interview was scheduled for three that afternoon; and when Audrey returned to the house on Lombard Street a little after five, her face was radiant. "I got the job, and I'll start next Monday, Aunt Margery!" she exulted. Dan Mason hadn't come home yet from the shop on O'Farrell Street, and he wasn't expected home until very late. He had stayed downtown last night until nearly eleven, going over the books with Fred Perry, explaining to his assistant just how he wanted to display and price the items he had bought in Honolulu, which would be shipped on a Matson freighter. He had seemed withdrawn and distracted upon his arrival, and Margery was getting a little worried about him because he looked so tired. After all, he hadn't taken a vacation at all this year, and he was at that time of life when a man should think of slowing down and getting plenty of rest and forgetting his business problems.

"That's wonderful, Audrey!" Margery Mason smiled. "What kind of job is it, and do you think you'll like it?"

"Well," Audrey confessed laughingly, "I'm just going to be a file clerk, at least for a few months until they see what I can do—that's what Mr. Beale says, anyway. And I'll start at sixty-five dollars a week. It's a wonderful location, a big insurance company on Montgomery Street, and there are some lovely little restaurants near there for lunch, and shops I've always wanted to visit. I think I'll have more fun than at school, really. And Aunt Margery, please, I want you to let me pay something for my room and board here. I really wouldn't feel right unless you let me do it. Next year I'll be of age, but I think I'm old enough now to make some decisions for myself."

"You're a very thoughtful, sweet girl, Audrey," Margery Mason replied, "but I for one don't intend to treat you like a boarder. You're family, after all, dear. Why, Beatrice looks upon you as a sister, and I think of you as a daughter, not just a cousin. So we'll have no more talk about such things unless you want to make me very cross."

Audrey came over to Margery Mason's chair, bent

down, and impulsively kissed her. "Thank you, Aunt Margery," she said softly. "Then we shan't talk about it. Except that one day, I'll try to do something nice for you and show you how very grateful I am."

But that day was never to come, because on the third Monday after Audrey had started her job at Blakeley & Beale, Margery Mason was stricken with a heart attack late in the afternoon and died en route to the hospital.

Chapter
TWELVE

THE FUNERAL had been at Cypress Lawn at three o'clock. Beatrice had driven her father and Audrey out to the cemetery, for Dan Mason was still in such a state of shock that it was wiser for him not to drive. He had stood there, numb, his face impassive, showing nothing of what he felt as the casket was lowered into the earth and then covered. There was a new headstone beside the one that marked Grover's grave, and Audrey had bought a little bouquet of violets to put on Grover's grave so that he would be remembered also. She had bought as well a wreath of white tuberoses to place on the grave of the woman whom she had called Aunt Margery and who had shown her as much affection these past thirteen years as it had been possible for Dan Mason's wife to show to anyone.

There had been a brittle, almost impersonal quality to her; there had been times, Audrey knew, even in the days when Grover had been the center of attention in the Mason household because of his athletic exploits, when it had seemed to her that Margery Mason had sat back and basked in that brief, reflected glory, as if she had expected nothing less. There had been few signs of affection all through the years between Grover and Beatrice and their mother, hardly more than Dan Mason himself had shown his offspring. They were not demonstrative as her own mother and Luka had been back on the island, but then this was a different world. All these years, it had been a world defined for her and limited within the walls of the stern old house on Lombard Street. It was a world that had no kinship with the one she had remembered in that other house thousands of miles across the blue Pacific.

And yet Margery Mason had been good to her, had been the only one ever to have kissed her and to have called her "dear" here on the mainland. It was strange now that she should think of this at the grave. For certainly Uncle Dan had never once kissed her, not even when she had been a little child looking to him in her fears and anxieties about beginning a new life in the house to which he had brought her. She had been lonely, lonelier than she had realized, and now beside the grave of Margery Mason she felt her own sense of loss. She would not soon forget Aunt Margery's kindness in bringing her along to visit Sue and Richard Wells last summer. That one act alone would have made her shed tears for the woman who now lay beside her son.

She turned now and saw Beatrice, wearing a black dress and veil, helping her father back along the walk. She was whispering to him, and he was nodding. Audrey wished that she could be beside him to comfort and console him. But her words would have little import for him in this desolate hour. He had only Beatrice left now, his own flesh and blood. She meant nothing to the old house any longer.

The evening of his return from Honolulu, he had called her into the library and told her that he had looked up the records in the Bureau of Conveyances and found nothing amiss. And then he had said a strange thing. "Before you can come into possession of this property, Audrey, I'm sure the court will expect to see the actual deed of sale which proves that your father bought the land and had clear title to it. I never found that document. Of course, the old records show that it's in Philip Mason's name. Naturally, I didn't check any further. But a friend of mine whose business is real estate told me how important it is to have the deed. Of course, it's more than a year away before we'll have to worry about it. And Luka and Hanale asked me to give you all their love. They're both fine, and they wish you well."

This was not the time to speak or even think of her inheritance. Not when the man who was her guardian was staggered and crushed by the suffering of his bereavement. She had briefly debated with herself, just before Aunt Margery's death, about the advisability of finding a room for herself somewhere near work, so that she would be totally independent and no longer a financial burden on Dan Mason. Now, it might be wiser to stay on, if only because her presence might help allay the loneliness of the house around him, just by knowing that she and Beatrice were there to comfort him and to look after his needs. To speak of paying for her room and board would be tactless also; instead, silently and without making any point of issue of it, she determined to take on herself many of Margery Mason's domestic chores. She had long ago learned how to cook and had often prepared her own meals when she had come home from school and found Aunt Margery out at some social function. Well, so long as she stayed on, she would cook the evening meals for Dan Mason and Beatrice and tidy up the house so that at least he and his daughter wouldn't be harassed by menial tasks. That would be her own token of paying him back for the years of bounty. She took a deep breath and followed them back to the car.

"I'll make supper for us, Bea," Audrey volunteered to her cousin as Dan Mason wearily inserted the key into the lock of the front door and turned it. He seemed to hesitate, as if reluctant to go in. Audrey's glance was compassionate and understanding.

"Thanks. That would be a help for sure. You can see how Daddy's taking this, and I don't think I'm up to any kitchen chores this evening," the redhead whispered back.

There was a silence to the house now, and outside, the sky was already gray and the first wispy hints of fog roll-

109

ing in from the ocean had begun to creep along the roofs of the houses higher up along Lombard Street. The curtains had been drawn over the spacious bay window of the living room, and there were bleakness and desolation everywhere. That illusion was further borne out by the utter absence of any pedestrians along the angling sidewalks, and at this moment of their return not even a single automobile was traveling along Lombard Street. Audrey could not help shivering as she turned on the threshold and looked back out upon the gloomy scene. Never since her arrival in San Francisco, she thought, had she yearned so much to see once again the sky and the ocean and the beautiful flowers of Hawaii.

She went directly to the roomy old kitchen, its huge gas range a relic from the days just after the great earthquake, and busied herself with the preparation of omelette and a tossed salad. The Masons had never had a maid, in spite of Margery Mason's penchant for social affairs; she had always managed to take full charge of all the domestic tasks, though to be sure there had been many an evening when the family had gone out to one of the fashionable restaurants if she found that the affair she was attending would stretch well toward evening. The kitchen was well arranged and spacious, and in the connecting pantry, far larger than its customary modern prototype, the narrow window afforded a view of the garden and the stone birdbath. As she went into the pantry to get some herbs for the omelette, Audrey stood for a moment looking out into the garden. The long shadows of twilight were falling now, and the stone birdbath took on an eerie shape as the shadows distorted its dull whiteness against the background of shrubs and tangled vines along the wall just beyond it. Not a bird twittered in that garden, not even a cricket chirped its friendly call. It was as if all life had deserted this sectioned-off enclosure, just as it had the house itself. Audrey drew a long breath and went back into the cheerfully lighted kitchen.

Dan Mason had slumped into the armchair, eyes closed, face drawn in the aftermath of this second irreparable loss. Beatrice, who had removed her veil, came over and bent to him, an arm around his shoulders. "Daddy, can't I do something for you?"

"No, darling. It's going to take a long while for me to get over this. I guess you really don't begin to miss someone and understand how much you've lost until they've gone. I thought when Grover died the world had ended, and now it's worse."

"Would you rather I didn't finish school and stayed home and took care of you, Daddy?"

Dan Mason straightened in his chair, uttered a long sigh, and turned to look at the provocative, red-haired young woman. "No, honey, but it's sweet of you to suggest it. I appreciate it more than you know, Beatrice."

She sank down on her knees, taking one of his hands and clasping it between her own, eyes intent on his tortured face. "I really don't care much about school any more. After all, I'm not going to be a career girl. And you needn't worry about my running off and getting married, either. There isn't anyone I've met I have the least interest in. I'd much rather just be your girl and be close to you, Daddy. There are just the two of us now, you know."

"But Audrey—" he began.

Beatrice shook her head, her lips tightening. "She's not really one of us, Daddy. You know that yourself. You've done everything for her all these years, but she still doesn't belong. She's different—you know what I mean. Oh, we get along all right, of course, and she's never really got in my way, or Grover's either. But I can't help resenting her just a little. When I think of how she's been able to manage for herself and not really take a part in anything we do, and then I think about Grover being gone—"

Dan Mason groaned, put his palm fiercely over Beatrice's mouth, and gasped, "For God's sake, don't! Don't talk like that, Beatrice."

She drew his hand away, then kissed it. Her eyes were narrowed, calculating, as she murmured, "But it's not fair, Daddy. After all, she's got another home to go to back where she was born. You said so yourself. And next year she'll inherit it, and then she'll skip off and be free of us, as if we never meant anything to her. And we don't, not really. It just isn't fair. I wish she weren't here—I wish she'd never been here, because I wanted you all to myself."

"But I've never kept anything from you, darling, I've never shown her more attention than you," he protested.

"I didn't mean to talk this way and hurt you, Daddy. It's only that we're so close now, and she's like a stranger here. She's taken everything and given nothing. Won't you let me stay home from school and look after you?"

Dan Mason took out his handkerchief, blew his nose, and then in a voice that strove to be cheerful, responded, "You're still my favorite girl, darling. Now let's forget all this. We mustn't show Audrey how unhappy we are. No, I want you to go on with the university and finish up in June. Maybe I'll have a nice graduation present for you. Maybe I'll let you take a cruise on the *Lurline* to Hawaii as your vacation present—would you like that?"

"Oh, yes, Daddy. That would be marvelous!" Beatrice gasped. She rose, kissed him on the forehead, and said, "I'll work very hard at school and make you proud of me. But you ought to go with me. The trip would do you a lot of good. Now let's get ready for supper. I feel better already, knowing that I'm your girl."

Beatrice went back to her classes the next day and Audrey to her office on Montgomery Street. Dan Mason, out of deference to his wife's memory, did not go back to his shop on O'Farrell Street until the following Monday. Then, as if to distract himself from his grief, he absorbed himself in work, and both Fred Perry and Flora Jenkins, the pleasant, mildly attractive salesclerk whose marriage to a now-dead scion from a distant branch of one of San Francisco's most prominent families had enabled her to draw many socialite customers to the shop, were kept extremely busy following his suggestions for repricing and changing the displays of merchandise.

Audrey did so well at her job that she received a small raise and a promotion to the rank of correspondent, her new task being to prepare letters to claimants and would-be policyholders. She said nothing more to Dan Mason about paying for her room and board, but many a Saturday morning she went to the grocery store and to the butcher shop to buy supplies, paying for them out of her own money, and preparing the meals and even tidying the ornate dust-catching furniture in the old house.

On the Friday of the last week in May, Audrey decided to spend her lunch hour walking down toward Fisherman's Wharf, perhaps eating in one of the numerous little restaurants along Taylor Street and enjoying the inimitable sourdough French bread (which no other city in the world except San Francisco can manage to bake because of the latter's unique climatic conditions) and accompanying this gastronomic treat with a dish of crabmeat, of which she was particularly fond.

She enjoyed just such a lunch, perched on a stool in front of a counter in one of the popular sidewalk cafés, and then strolled on down Taylor Street, pausing in front of the shop windows to admire their displays, which vied with the colorful street stalls where buckets of live crabs and strings of huge sponges clamored for the attention of the passersby. On the corner of Jefferson and Taylor, she stopped in front of The Captain's Sea Chest, one of the oldest and most famous shops in the area and a perennial favorite with the tourists. It was a bright, warm, sunny day, and Audrey felt a sense of keen gratitude for the contrast between the bustling street and the almost unendurable solemnity and quiet of the house on Lombard Street. She caught a reflection of her own face in the glass window of the shop, her glossy black hair flowing in a thick pageboy whose curls caressed her slim shoulders, her eyes wide as those of a child that wakes early on a Christmas morning and hurries down to in-

113

spect the packages under the tree. And she was smiling, she reflected, as she had seldom smiled of late. The job had been a godsend for her. Everyone was so friendly, so helpful. She had concentrated on her work and tried to learn the routine as quickly as possible, so that she might be useful. Now, in a relatively short time, she felt herself accepted as an associate. In thirteen years, she had achieved less identification with those who had brought her up from childhood; it was too morbid a paradox on which to ponder this enchanting, fresh May day.

She glanced at the inexpensive little Westclox wristwatch she had recently bought herself. It would soon be time to go back to the office. The other girls never seemed to care whether they were five, ten, or even fifteen minutes late back from lunch, and nothing was really ever said, so long as they did their work. Yet she felt a scrupulous honesty about her employer's time. She would allow herself five minutes to browse inside, no more.

As she reached for the door, a man's hand turned the knob ahead of her. "May I, please?" his strong, resonant voice asked.

"Oh—thank you." Audrey smiled and entered the shop. She couldn't help thinking, after a quick glance she had given him, that he was extremely handsome. At least six feet tall, sturdily built, with a frank, smiling face and pleasant blue eyes. He had black hair, and he seemed tanned as if from the sun. She walked toward the side of the shop to inspect the display of picture postcard folders neatly arranged in the little revolving rack. There was one there of Hawaii, and she took it out and examined it. Impulsively, she walked toward the nearby counter where a salesclerk was waiting on customers and purchased the folder and dropped it into her purse. It was really time to be going back now, but she had to have one last look. There were so many lovely things here that one could spend an entire day looking at them and yet not see everything.

In the center of the shop, there was a rectangular glass

114

case, presided over by a smiling, gray-haired, bespectacled clerk. Along the top of the case were handsome little baskets and trays of seashells, while in the case below, neatly packaged in ornamental boxes and resting on cotton beds, were cowrie and conch shells of all types, with their breathtaking range of colors from a pastel brown to a violent vermillion.

Transfixed, Audrey stopped before the case, her eyes drawn toward one of the boxes in which reposed a huge conch shell, nacreous like mother of pearl, with intricate whorls and knobs and a spiraled top. Alongside it were other boxes containing the delicate miter from the coral reefs, spindle shells found in pairs on the sandy bottoms, the delicately sculptured, alabaster-white latiaxis from the deep waters around Japan, the gaudy pink-mouthed Murex that had once been used as a source of dye by the Phoenicians, and the brown Delphinula whose horny operculum was sharpened on the Indo-Pacific reefs.

"May I help you, Miss?" the clerk asked.

"Might I see that giant conch, please?"

"Of course." The clerk slid aside the glass doors to the case, reached in, brought out the box, and laid it on the counter before Audrey. Gently, almost reverently, she lifted it, examining it, then held it to her ear. And the mystic roar of the ocean was summoned up. The years fell back, and she was again on Waimanalo Beach. The conch . . . that last day on the island, when Luka had told her that she must keep the secret of the conch buried under the papaya tree, the secret that would prove that the land and the house belonged to her now that her parents were gone. Uncle Dan had said that he could not find the paper proving her father's ownership. That must have been what Luka meant that last day in the garden. And Luka had said that she must tell no one of the secret.

All these years that warning had lingered with her, though she had never felt the need for such secrecy. Yet now, suddenly, holding the conch to her ear, remembering Luka's insistence, it all came back so clearly. Had

115

Luka feared that someone would try to take away the house and the land her parents meant to leave her? Surely Uncle Dan, who had been so good to her, would never think of such a thing. Yet Luka had taken her into the garden while he had waited in the cab and had made her promise never to reveal to anyone the secret of the conch shell. She would keep the secret. Besides, in a few more months she would come of age, and then it would be time enough to find the paper.

"Isn't it a magnificent conch?" She had laid it back down into its bed of cotton as he spoke. Turning, she recognized the man who had opened the door for her. "It's beautiful," she agreed. "I'd love to have it, but I'll have to come back some other time. I'll be late back to the office as it is."

"You know, in Hawaii they summon guests to the *luau* by blowing on just such a conch," the man said to her.

"Why, that's right." Audrey smiled. "But they don't have *luaus* here in San Francisco, I'm afraid."

He chuckled, showing strong white teeth and a friendly smile. "You're quite right. But they do where I come from, back in Honolulu. My name is Kamaki Marshall."

"I'm glad to meet you, Mr. Marshall. My name is Audrey Mason. You live in Honolulu?"

"Well, rather more on the windward side of Oahu. But my work is in Honolulu. Audrey Mason, you say? Then back in Hawaii they would call you Aukele."

She stared at him for a moment, her eyes widening. The way he had pronounced that name by which her mother and Luka had called her made the years roll back. She had almost forgotten how it sounded, since no one in the house on Lombard Street had ever called her that.

"I—I really have to be getting back to the office, Mr. Marshall. It's been very nice meeting you. Perhaps I'll see you again someday."

He smiled and nodded. "Till then, *aloha, a hui hou kaua,* good wishes till we meet again."

116

She was mute, could only nod acknowledgment. For those were almost the very same words that Luka had used to bid her farewell on the day when Uncle Dan had come to take her back with him. How strange it was that her impulse had taken her to this shop and to this meeting. How strange that she should have been drawn here to find the conch shell that reminded her of Luka and the secret.

He stood watching her as she opened the door, and her cheeks colored with an exquisite confusion, knowing that he was watching. Then she hurried back up Taylor Street. This would be the first time that she had ever been late for work.

In her haste, she did not notice a young, red-haired woman in a chic green rayon frock who was standing on the opposite corner. Nor did she see how Beatrice Mason turned to watch her as she made her way through the crowds until at last she disappeared from view. And long after she had vanished, Beatrice Mason stood looking, her eyes narrowed and her lips compressed. It was neither a look of amity nor of surprise. It was rather a look of impregnable hostility. Yet a few moments later, when the tall, black-haired young man left the shop and began to stroll down the crowded street, the look on Beatrice Mason's provocative, sensuous face became altered to one of open admiration.

Chapter
THIRTEEN

BEATRICE MASON walked quickly into the dining room, went over to her father, and kissed him. "You look terribly tired, Daddy. But maybe that's a good sign if it means that business is getting better again."

Dan Mason shook his head and uttered a weary sigh. "I wish it was, honey. I just don't know what's got into this town any more. Looks to me as if the Chamber of Commerce ought to do something about easing some of the restrictions so the conventioneers would be more inclined to stop here instead of going down to Los Angeles. I've never seen such a puritanical administration in all the years I've lived here."

"Why, what's wrong now, Daddy?" Beatrice straightened, an arm round his shoulders, fondly looking down at him. The long rectangular cherrywood table seemed empty indeed with only three chairs placed before it. Her chair was at her father's right, and Audrey's was at the left. Her fingers convulsively tightened against her father's shoulder; that was where Grover had used to sit. It wasn't right at all, somehow, that Audrey should be there.

Dan Mason uttered another sigh. "Well, just as an example, last fall the mayor had the chief of police close down the Blackhawk on the grounds that it wasn't a safe place for teenagers. You know, for years they've had jazz concerts there, with a screened-off section where the teenagers sit. And they've never served them anything there but soft drinks; they're very strict about it. And then when the African Ballet came to town, the city fathers wanted the women dancers to wear brassieres. We talk about our culture and our sophistication, and the people of Los Angeles just laugh at us and get all the business. No, it looks like another slow summer."

"It'll be all right, dear. Don't you worry so. What you really ought to do is to come along with me to Hawaii. Oh . . ." She bent down to press her cheek against his and in a coaxing voice, purred, "Maybe I oughtn't to think about being so extravagant if business isn't good, Daddy."

His hand gently stroked the back of her neck. "Now don't you even start to think about anything like that, sweetheart. I've already reserved passage on the *Lurline* for June twenty-seventh, the week after your classes are over. All you have to worry about is packing and having a good time."

"But I wouldn't want to go alone without you, Daddy," she protested.

"I'll send Audrey along with you. I've reserved a double room on the upper deck for the two of you."

Beatrice drew back, her face cold and hostile. "I don't see why you want to do that, Daddy. She hasn't earned a vacation like that, and this was to be my graduation present. I'd so much rather go with you."

"There's a reason for my wanting Audrey to accompany you, darling," Dan Mason explained. "She'll be of age in a few months, and as her guardian before I can turn over the property her father left, it's important that I have the original deed of sale. I wasn't able to find it when I searched the house before, and this woman Luka couldn't tell me anything about it. I've always had a feeling that Luka told Audrey when they were alone together just where the deed was, and perhaps Audrey has forgotten. I'm sure that if she goes back to the house on the beach she can find it—and you can help her, of course."

"I see. Oh, I nearly forgot, Daddy. There's another let-

120

ter for you from that man in Honolulu. I left it on the hall table. I'll get it right away." Beatrice gave him a hug, then left the room and returned in a few moments with an airmail letter. Dan Mason took it with a nod, glanced up to make sure that he was alone with Beatrice, then quickly opened it. It read as follows:

Esteemed señor Mason:

I hope that all is well with you and your family. You will remember that I told you I might have a buyer for the property which we discussed. It now appears that a very important person from the mainland, who builds housing projects and apartments, has looked over the property and tells me that within the next few years it is quite likely to be an ideal site for a luxury residential hotel apartment building. He would be willing to pay $80,000 for clear title at the present time.

This is speculative, of course. You may decide to wait for a higher price, but on the other hand, you may lose the immediate interest of this very solvent buyer. Also, as I know that you are holding this property in trust for your ward, she may not wish to sell when she comes into legal ownership of it. Therefore it would be well to act quickly if this proposition interests you. I suggest that you telephone me to save time, and I can then acquaint you with a procedure which I believe would be to your *great* advantage.

I look forward to hearing from you as quickly as possible. Till then, my most cordial greetings.

In the next to last paragraph of that letter, the word "great" had been underlined. And the signature was that of Estaban Aguinaldo. Dan Mason cleared his throat, nervously glanced up again to see whether Audrey had returned from the kitchen, then folded the letter and put it into his inside coat pocket. Beatrice was staring at him, a questioning little smile on her insolent mouth.

121

He had almost forgotten what a mature and beautiful young woman she had become. With her red hair coiled in a coronet braid around the top of her head, standing in an attitude of imperious self-sufficiency, she had many of her mother's traits. Like her mother, she was ambitious; Margery had wanted social prominence and recognition from the elite. He himself had never quite been able to give it to her. But Beatrice had more than Margery's pretentions; she had determination and strength that would achieve whatever she sought. If only poor Grover had had some of that unwavering determination, he would be alive today, Dan Mason sorrowfully thought.

"Good news, Daddy?" Beatrice asked.

"Very possibly. Now why don't you go out to the kitchen and see if you can help your Cousin Audrey. We'll talk about the trip to Honolulu after supper." Absently, Dan Mason touched his coat at the place where the letter rested.

Audrey had prepared a chicken salad the night before, after having washed and put away the supper dishes. She served it now with piping-hot biscuits and tall glasses of iced tea to which she had added sprigs of mint. "I hope you'll like this, Uncle Dan," she said as she set an individual bowl of salad down before him. Beatrice grimaced with distaste. "I know it's summery and all that," she declaimed with the petulant tone of one who has been denied expectations, "but it would be nice to have a steak some night, don't you think, Audrey?"

"Yes, it would, Bea," Audrey frankly retorted as she set the redhead's salad bowl in front of her, "but it's much too expensive these days, and it isn't very good in flavor."

"You're a fine one to talk about economizing," Beatrice sniffed as she gingerly dipped her fork into the salad bowl. "Daddy practically took you away from a desert island and brought you up and gave you the best of everything."

"That's enough, Beatrice!" Dan Mason intervened, his face crisp with outrage. And yet the sharpness of his tone was in part subconsciously prompted by his secret agreement with the thought his daughter had just expressed. Yes, he had given Philip's child everything, denied her nothing, and now with Grover and Margery gone, she was actually better off than either one of them. "Besides"—his voice was gentle now, as he tried to put an end to this cousinly bickering—"it won't do for the two of you to be on bad terms if you're going to share the same stateroom."

Audrey, who had taken her place at the table, and had silently begun to eat her meal without responding to Beatrice's hostile jibe, looked up in surprise. "What do you mean, Uncle Dan?"

He laid down his fork. "Well, I hadn't meant to say anything until after we've finished supper, but I guess I've let the cat out of the bag, Audrey. You see, I promised Beatrice a trip to Honolulu on the *Lurline* as a combination birthday and graduation present. And I'd like you to go along with her, Audrey. You know, we talked about the land that your father left you, and how I'll have to have the deed in order to have the courts recognize your claim. I think it would be an excellent idea if you went along with Beatrice and searched the house to find it. Perhaps Luka can help you."

"But didn't you tell me, Uncle Dan, that the records showed that my father owned the property?" Audrey asked wonderingly.

"That's true, my dear. But it's been a very long time, since before the war, you see. And Hawaii has become a state in the meantime. To avoid legal complications, it would be very wise to find the deed and to let me have it so that when you become twenty-one this October, you can come into your estate without any trouble."

"I—I'd love to see Honolulu again, Uncle Dan. But I've just started my new job, and I don't know if they'd let me go."

"I'm sure they will, my dear. If you wish, I can call your employers and tell them the circumstances."

"Oh no, please, Uncle Dan, I'd much rather you didn't. I'll ask for myself, I think that's the proper thing to do.

It's very good of you to offer me such a wonderful trip."
She shook her head with a rueful smile. "I'd be telling a
fib if I said I didn't want to go, because I do, so very
much."

"Then it's settled. You and Beatrice will sail June
twenty-seventh. I think if you ask your employers to let
you have two or three weeks off for such a trip, they
won't mind. The summer is a slack time in the insurance
business, I'm sure, with everyone going away on vacation.
And it would be nice for Beatrice to have a companion.
I shan't go, because I want to look after the shop."

"Thank you so much, Uncle Dan. But a trip on that
beautiful liner costs so much—I oughtn't to accept it
from you."

Beatrice gave her cousin another spiteful glance. "You
don't have to be mealy-mouthed, Audrey. Daddy's just
generous, that's his way. Anyway, if you feel it costs so
much, you can always pay him back when you get that
land your father left you."

"Beatrice!" Dan Mason exclaimed, swiftly gesturing
to his daughter to drop the subject.

But the redhead cattily persisted. "To look at Audrey,
Daddy, you'd never guess what a consummate actress she
is. Never goes out with boys, works hard in the kitchen,
gives up school so she can get a job. Only you don't see
her all the time. Tell me, Audrey, who is that handsome
hunk of man you were flirting with this noon down there
in that curio shop on Taylor Street?"

Audrey gasped, her face flaming. "That's not true, Bea!
I went into the shop to look at the shells, and he happened to be standing there and started to talk to me. And
then he held the door open for me, and that's all it was.
You haven't any right to say such nasty things."

"Well, I'll say this for you, for a girl who's never shown
any interest in fellows, you certainly picked a winner
this time, Audrey. For once, I'd have to go along with
your taste," Beatrice Mason said wickedly. Then, catching her father's irate glance, she giggled softly and resumed eating. A moment later, as a kind of afterthought

she added, "Oh, by the way, Daddy, I didn't know Mr. Perry rode cabs during his lunch hour."

"What are you talking about, Beatrice?"

"Why, Daddy, you know I had only one morning class today, so I went downtown to have lunch with Kitty Price, and we wound up at Caesar's for lasagna. Then we decided to walk along Fisherman's Wharf, and that's how I saw Audrey flirting with her new boyfriend."

"That isn't true, and you know it!" Audrey flashed, her cheeks crimsoning again.

"What's this about Fred Perry?" Dan Mason curtly interrupted. "He always eats at David's, so far as I know."

"Maybe he does, Daddy, but just the same Kitty and I saw him in a cab that was going over to the North Beach area. He looked very excited, and he was fiddling with his bow tie." She giggled again. "Maybe he was sneaking off to meet a lady love, even at his age."

"Beatrice, I'm afraid I don't appreciate your sarcastic vein this evening. Fred Perry is the last man in the world I'd suspect of having a girlfriend. He's lived with his old-maid sister all these years, his habits are as regular as clockwork, and he's a dutiful and industrious worker. I owe him a great deal, and he's never taken advantage of me. His judgment about what will sell is practically as good as mine. I have no intention of asking him why he took a cab during his noon hour, so we'll have no more of that." He tasted a mouthful of chicken salad, then almost patronizingly said to Audrey, "This is quite good, my dear. You're looking after us very well, I must say."

After she had washed and put away the dishes, Audrey went upstairs to her room. Beatrice's sly remarks about her chance meeting with Kamaki Marshall had nettled her, and she tried without success to read a book. Finally, distraught, she laid the book down on the bed, opened the door of her room, and went down the hall to the dormer whose window looked out onto Lombard Street. The evening was cool, but this time there was hardly any fog, and the street lamps glowed with a bright fervor. An automobile went by, slowly descending toward the artery that would connect it with the main section of the city. Across the street, someone was pulling down the shade of the second-floor living-room window. The street seemed deserted again, and even the bright light of the streetlamps did not banish the grotesque shadows cast by the narrow houses and apartments huddled together so closely that it seemed that they were all part of a single sprawling edifice. She raised the window a little to let in the cool air, for the dormer was stuffy. As she did so, she heard the sound of footsteps, slow, deliberate, coming from the left, and she turned her head to see.

The footsteps came closer, and now she could see that it was a tall young man, black-haired, wearing a light spring overcoat, his head and shoulders poised, his body leaning forward at the angle pedestrians in San Francisco seem to take from birth when ascending one of the steep streets of the city. As he reached the gateway leading to the steps and the veranda, he stopped and turned to look up at the house. She started, eyes widening with recognition. It was Kamaki Marshall, the man she had met in The Captain's Sea Chest. He stood for several minutes looking at the house, then slowly turned and went back down the street, disappearing from view, swallowed up by the shadows.

It was all so strange. Why had he come to this house? She had told him only her name, nothing more. There was no doubt that it was he, the man who had spoken to her about the conch shell and the *luau*. Who was he? What unerring instinct had brought him to the house where she lived? It could not be by chance, or he would have gone on along the street, not stopped and then gone back whence he had come, after looking at the house. Or again, someone might have told him about this house, about her. But who, and why?

He had said that he came from Honolulu, or rather, that he worked in Honolulu and lived in Oahu. And this same evening Uncle Dan had asked her again to find the deed to the house on Waimanalo Beach. Was it all a sign, the coincidental meeting at the shop on Taylor Street and then this young man's walking to the house and then going away?

Luka had told her to keep the secret. She knew now that she would not tell even Uncle Dan where that all-important paper was hidden. For she knew that there was no other living heir, no other child born to Milliama and Philip Mason. And if, as Uncle Dan had told her, records in Honolulu showed that her father had clear title to the property on Waimanalo Beach, she did not think it was nearly so vital as he made out for him to have that document in his possession. Unless . . . unless this mysterious, handsome stranger who had accosted her this noon had some unknown claim that would dispute her own.

Chapter
FOURTEEN

A MILD COLD kept Dan Mason confined to the house Monday and Tuesday of the first week of June. Audrey, before going off to work at the insurance office, made him as comfortable as she could by preparing his breakfast and bringing it in to him on a tray and setting forth on the little night table a bottle of the cold pills he had used with some success in years past. He grumblingly complained that the advent of summer was treacherous in San Francisco, because if you dressed lightly during the end of May when the sun was warm, you forgot about the cold, foggy nights that always settled in. Invariably his colds had come this same time of year.

Audrey made some glasses of fruit juice and left them in the refrigerator for his use during the day, told him to get as much rest as he could, and went off to work. Beatrice looked in on him when she came back from the university and exclaimed that she wouldn't think of taking a pleasure cruise when he was so sick. Dan Mason found it rather pleasant, for all his outward grumpiness, to be fussed over by the two attractive young women.

He felt so much better on Wednesday that he insisted on going to the shop, though Audrey warned him not to get chilled, because the cold would only settle in and give him a long siege. He told her that he would take a cab to the shop, have it wait for him while he made sure that everything was in order, and then come right back home.

However, everything was definitely not in order when he walked into the shop on O'Farrell Street. Flora Jenkins hurried up to him, wringing her hands, her voice trembling with anxiety. "Oh, Mr. Mason, I was just going to call your house. I've been so worried!"

"Why, what's the matter? Where's Fred?"

"That's what I was going to call you about, Mr. Mason," Flora Jenkins stammered, nervously glancing about as the little bells above the door tinkled to announce the entry of a customer.

He made a gesture with his hand and whispered, "Take care of her, will you? I'll go back into the office, and we can talk it over quietly after you've finished your sale."

The back room of the shop was neatly arranged, with sectional shelves providing storage space for replacements of standard merchandise, a wide clearing at the back for incoming cartons and crates, and a work table conveniently near the rear door. To the right was a small partitioned office with desk, swivel chair, and file cabinets, as well as a small floor safe in which Dan Mason kept the day's receipts. Fred Perry banked these every morning, so that no more than a full day's take was ever locked up in the safe overnight.

The storage room was certainly a model of neatness and orderliness, he thought, an exact reflection of Fred Perry's own life. Fred and his sister had several times invited him and Margery over to dinner at their apartment on the Avenue, and he had often remarked to Margery that the Perry abode was incontrovertible proof that a wild party had never been thrown there, for not even an ashtray was out of place, nor the corner of a rug rumpled. The only sign of real use was the bookcase in Fred Perry's bedroom, for the books inside it showed that they had been read and re-read many times, judging from the broken spines of some of the volumes and the little tabs of paper Perry had stuck in between pages to mark places to which he meant to return.

On the desk in front of him was a plain white envelope

with his own name written on it. He recognized the handwriting as being that of his chief assistant and was just about to open it, when Flora Jenkins came hurriedly into the back room and stood before him, clasping her hands and twisting her slender fingers in a feverish agitation.

"Now what's all this excitement about, Flora? Where's Fred?" he repeated.

"Mr. Mason, you know that Mr. Perry has been here a very long time, and you've always trusted him," she began, her face reddening as he stared at her, waiting for her to go on.

"Certainly I know that. He's had thirty years with me. Now what's upset you so?"

"Well, it's not my place to spy on anybody, Mr. Mason, but Fred has been acting very strangely the last few weeks. I didn't think anything of it, but then yesterday he said he was going to the bank in the afternoon. He almost always goes in the morning, as you know."

"Yes, as regularly as clockwork. So perhaps he got busy in the shop and didn't have a chance to get to the bank, for once. That's no reason to be alarmed."

"No, sir, except that he hasn't come back. I mean, he left yesterday afternoon and he didn't come back at all and he hasn't called. And now he isn't here at all today. And when I called his apartment this morning, because I thought maybe he was sick, his sister said she hadn't seen him since yesterday morning, Mr. Mason."

"That's certainly odd. Well, let me worry about it, Flora. You go back to the store. You know I never like to have it empty at any time."

"Yes, sir. I do hope nothing's happened," she quavered.

At that moment, the tinkle of the little Japanese bells announced another customer. Flora Jenkins gasped and hurried back to her post behind the counter. Dan Mason picked up the envelope. It was heavier than a letter should be, and his fingers felt a thick, rectangular enclosure. Adjusting his pince-nez with a frown, he slit open the envelope. Inside, he found a Bank of America deposit book, with the name of the shop, MASON IMPORTS, printed in gold on the black cloth. There were four folded sheets, which he at once opened and read. At the very first paragraph, his jaw dropped in the incredulous expression of dazed bewilderment.

Dear Mr. Mason:

I know that you will think that I am a thief, but I must assure you that what I am doing is not at all criminal, because I intend to return the money to you, not only with interest, but with a handsome return on this investment. On the other hand, this imminent return cannot be possible unless I have the investment to make, and it is not for a cause which has anything to do with gambling or women, I assure you. I have worked for you faithfully for thirty years, and you know my honesty.

You see, Mr. Mason, I have led a very lonely life, devoting all of it to my work in the store. You have never had till now any reason to question my conduct, and this is why I hope you will be understanding and tolerant about what I have done. Some months ago, quite by accident, I met a man named Louis Maraschin, who has a flower shop on Irving and Ninth Avenue. I found him a most extraordinary man, and went there several times to buy my sister flowers. We became good friends, and he told me something of his life. He was the victim of a dishonest brother who robbed him of his own inheritance. He worked for some years as a laborer, then as a taxicab driver, until he saved enough to open a florist shop. Seeking truth and spiritual inspiration after the tragedies which had befallen him, he studied spiritualism and became an ordained minister.

Reverend Maraschin took me into his confidence a month ago, and told me that he had befriended a man who had once been one of the most important figures in America's financial history. This man, he explained, had been one of the pool operators during the time of the Teapot Dome investigation, a great scandal back in the twenties. He himself was simply an innocent bystander, not knowing what chicanery the big oil companies were practicing. When the facts were publicized, the Secret Service at once arrested him and confiscated his property and his money, and even after he had been cleared by court investigation, he and his wife were constantly harassed by private detectives and Secret Service men who would visit their apartment at any time of the day or night.

This man, Reverend Maraschin told me, turned to drink to forget his sufferings. But the Supreme Powers saw in him a medium whereby They might transmit to all mankind Their immortal messages. This man's name was Philip Hackett, and Reverend Maraschin took him into his own tiny little apartment, fed him, and cared for him. Also, when Hackett was stricken with fever and delirium—or so Reverend Maraschin thought at the time—he would talk aloud, using the most beautiful language ever to pass between the lips of a mortal man. So impressed was Reverend Maraschin with this that he faithfully transcribed all of Hackett's manifestations —for so they were. There were writings enough to fill scores of printed volumes, all containing the wisdom of the ages which will guide mankind out of the darkness and the jungle of hatred and bigotry.

Reverend Maraschin let me read these wonderful effusions and showed me how several of the plots of great plays which had come from the Supreme Powers through Philip Hackett's brain had been perniciously stolen by Hollywood movie producers, who did not pay a cent of royalty. I am of the opinion, Mr. Mason, that these writings must be made available to a world which has turned away from righteousness and which regards only material things as meaningful. So Reverend Maraschin and I are going to Mexico with this money I have borrowed from you, and there we shall found a publishing press of our own to disseminate these great teachings. I am certain that the sales will be so great as to enable me to pay you back in full what I have borrowed, as well as a fair share of the profits.

It has been a privilege to have worked for you all this time, and believe me, Mr. Mason, if it were not that late in life I have stumbled upon the Eternal Secrets, I should be content to end my days as an employee in your shop. Do not think badly of me, because I have every intention of repaying you, and more.

Yours most sincerely,
Fred Perry

Dan Mason's lips moved convulsively as the typed sheets fell from his nerveless hands. Then slowly he opened the bankbook, which had been established as a sole proprietorship and to which Fred Perry's signature had been added some fifteen years ago with the power of depositing and issuing checks drawn upon the store's funds. Last week, there had been a balance of $12,978.38, but now there was only a little over $2,000. The bank, of course, had not questioned Fred Perry's withdrawal, since his identity and right to issue checks as well as deposit them had been so long established.

With property taxes on the house on Lombard Street, the rental of the shop, and Flora Jenkins's wages, the balance in the bankbook would just about be wiped out.

He sat there staring at the bankbook, the muscles of his jaw flexing in his savage effort to keep control. Then he picked up the bankbook again and looked at the entry of withdrawal. There was no mistake about it. By this time Fred Perry would easily be across the Mexican border with the money. There was no clue to what part of that colorful and mysterious country his employee might have gone; it would be utterly futile to attempt to bring him back, though of course he would notify the San Francisco police and ask them to communicate with the Mexican authorities. There were so many remote provinces, so many tiny towns not even on the map, in which Fred Perry and this florist-spiritualist could hide themselves.

What an irony it was, Dan Mason thought, to have counted so much on the reliability of habit, the predictability of routine. Of all the people in the world, he would have sworn that Fred Perry would have lived out the rest of his days content with his lot, happy in the little world of being responsible for invoices and incoming shipments, for bank deposits and displays of stock to attract customers. Content with his books and his placid, cheerless life with his sister. He would have understood it better if it had been gambling or women, or perhaps the desperate hope of having a last fling, like taking a trip around the world before he died. These would have been calculable aberrations, and there would have been signs of them long since in Fred Perry's conduct about the shop. But until this moment when Flora Jenkins had told him of Perry's mystifying disappearance, in all those thirty years of service and self-effacing loyalty, there had not been the faintest clue to herald this sudden and dramatic leavetaking. And it came at the most intolerable of times, when his debts were heavy and his income from the shop certain to be scant during the oncoming summer months; when he had already invested nearly fifteen hundred dollars in the *Lurline* trip for Beatrice and for Audrey as her companion, with at least another five hundred dollars to be given Beatrice for her expenses in Honolulu. It would mean replacing the money out of his own personal savings account, which itself was none too healthy. And if the fall season did not show an improvement in business, it could very likely mean ruin for him.

He read Fred Perry's letter again, from the beginning, word by word, trying to glean from it those facets of character which he had not guessed about Fred Perry. Yet it

135

was always the same. With all his shrewdness and business judgment, he had understood his most trusted employee no better than he had his own son. For a moment, with no one around to see this concession to weakness, Dan Mason bowed his head on his folded arms and uttered an inarticulate groan. He had never felt such helplessness, such futility.

Then, recovering, he reached for the phone, dialed the number of the police, and in a low, level voice asked for an officer to come to his shop so that he might prefer a charge of grand theft against one of his employees. Then he went out into the shop to tell Flora Jenkins that when the officer came, she was to send him directly back into the office. He did not tell her what Fred Perry's letter had said.

When it was noon and the officer had come and gone with the information Dan Mason had given him, the gray-haired importer sent the stunned and wondering Flora Jenkins out to lunch. For the hour that she was gone, he stood behind the counter, waiting on occasional customers who came to browse rather more than to buy. The activity helped distract his mind from the shattering blow he had just received, gave him time to crystallize his thoughts into a plan of action. No, even if Fred Perry could be found and extradited, it would take a long time and a good deal of money. And he had no assurance that even if Fred Perry were found, the ten thousand dollars would be recovered. Meanwhile, there were bills to be met, and expenses would go on apace.

Flora Jenkins returned promptly at one o'clock and replaced her employer behind the counter. Dan Mason went back to his office. He had turned over the bankbook and the letter to a police officer. He stared again around the neatly arranged back room. Its orderliness was testimony to Fred Perry's efficiency and devotion to his work. He shook his head slowly, as if it were a nightmare from which he was just waking. Then slowly he picked up the phone and dialed long distance. The operator had to identify herself several times before he finally

136

spoke. And then, in a hoarse voice he himself did not recognize, he said, "I want to call Honolulu. Mr. Estaban Aguinaldo. The telephone number is three three one, nine six. Please put it through as quickly as you can."

He waited while the circuit was being completed, till the sound of the ringing signal in Honolulu came to his ears. Then there was a click, and a voice responding, "This is Aguinaldo, good morning."

"This is Dan Mason here in San Francisco," he said, his voice noticeably trembling. "I have decided to go ahead with the proposition we have discussed. Yes, I'll arrange for an advance fee at once. And I'll write you an explanatory letter. You're sure that it can be done? I'm relying on you. Goodbye."

When he replaced the phone, his forehead was damp with sweat and his hand was trembling. After a long moment, he got up from the desk, went over to the safe, and dialed the combination. Opening it, he took out a teakwood box, exquisitely carved. Sliding back the lid, he disclosed a chess set made of magnificent dark green jade. He had picked it up in Hong Kong just before his marriage, on the occasion of the very first business trip with which his father had entrusted him. He had bought it for a mere four hundred dollars; now it was worth at least ten times that much. One of his competitors over on Sansome Street had often tried to buy it from him. Well, he was going to sell it. And the money would be turned into a bank draft that would be forwarded to the little Filipino realtor whom he had met at the Queen's Surf last fall. . . .

It was nearly four o'clock in the afternoon, nearly time for the big Matson luxury liner to pull up anchor. Beatrice and Audrey were saying their goodbyes in their stateroom, where the genial little Hawaiian steward had already placed their luggage. Audrey could not hide her excitement at the thought of seeing the island of Oahu for the first time in nearly fourteen years. Yet once again she felt deeply obligated to her father's cousin.

She glanced around at the luxurious appointments of this spacious double room, with its individually controlled air-conditioning thermostat, the richly and colorfully uphostered chairs and Pullman couch, and the wide, round tabouret with its gleaming Formica top and lustrous walnut legs. There was a huge bouquet of white and red chrysanthemums in a vase on the mirrored dressing table. And on the tabouret Dan Mason had placed a five-pound box of Mrs. See's mouthwatering chocolate creams. Despite Dan Mason's cordial insistence that he wished her to accompany Beatrice as a companion on this pleasure trip, Audrey could not help feeling like a poor relation to whom largesse had been condescendingly given.

Dan Mason adjusted his pince-nez and glanced about the room with a smile. "There's the whistle for going ashore," he said. "Well, I've made sure the steward will take good care of both of you. Enjoy yourselves, as I'm sure you will. Beatrice darling, as soon as you dock in Honolulu, I want you to call me. That should be a little after ten in the morning next Friday. I've reserved a double room for you both at the Royal Hawaiian. Beatrice, that was where your mother and I spent our honeymoon. I want you to remember her and to say a prayer for her."

The red-haired girl kissed her father warmly. "Daddy, this is just about the most wonderful birthday present any girl had. I can't thank you enough. I only wish you were going along with us."

"That's right," Dan Mason chuckled, patting his daughter's shoulder, "your birthday and your graduation from the university came at about the same time, didn't they? All the more reason for this trip. I've given you a kind of itinerary, Beatrice. There are some wonderful restaurants you and Audrey will want to try and some particularly beautiful scenic spots you must visit. It's all outlined in this letter. And I've enclosed a prescription for sleeping tablets from Doctor Haller, my dear. I told him how hard it's been for you to get to sleep the past few weeks. But the trip should help relax you." He reached into his lapel pocket and drew out an envelope. "And there's something even more practical inside the envelope, too, darling. Expense money while you're on the island."

"Thank you ever so much, Daddy!" Beatrice hugged him and kissed him again, "I'll be sure to call you just as soon as we land."

"Good. Well, I'd better get off or they'll sail with me, and I don't have a ticket." He gave Beatrice a last affectionate hug, then walked toward the door of the stateroom. "Audrey, my dear, remember what we've talked about concerning the deed to your father's property. I hope you'll make every effort to find it while you're on the island. Perhaps Luka may remember where your father put it. As I told you, when I went back there last fall, I looked in the secretary, but I couldn't find it anywhere. And it's most important that I have it."

"Yes, Uncle Dan, I'll try to find it," Audrey replied dutifully. "I'm terribly grateful to you for sending me along with Beatrice. And I do mean to pay you back. Though I really feel guilty about taking time away from my work, since I really haven't been on the job long enough to have earned a vacation."

"Nonsense, my dear." His tone was unusually affable. "I took the liberty of telephoning your employer just after we had our little chat. He was delighted to know that you were going back to the place where you were born, and he spoke very highly of your work. I'm sure he hasn't any feeling that you didn't earn a vacation. And we shan't talk of payment, remember. It's my pleasure —and too, you're earning your passage by being Beatrice's companion. She wouldn't have half so much fun if she went alone. Well, as they say on the Islands, *aloha*." He leaned toward Audrey and kissed her on the cheek.

"Thank you again for everything, Uncle Dan," she murmured.

139

He turned in the doorway and waved to them both, then strode down the corridor, as the final all-ashore whistle sounded its prolonged wail.

Beatrice walked over to the closet, opened it, and chose a smart magenta-hued frock. "I don't know about you," she said, "but I'm going to that *malihini* cocktail dance. My friend Cynthia, who's made this trip lots of times, says the Hawaiian Trio has the most wonderful rhythm for dancing." She held up the dress against herself and added with a mocking smile, "It's too bad you really don't have much of a wardrobe for a trip like this, Audrey dear."

"There's nothing wrong with the dress I'm wearing, Beatrice," Audrey responded calmly. "I don't think I'll be too much out of place. I'll go with you, if you dont mind."

"Oh, no, not at all," Beatrice retorted airily as she began to change dresses. "After all, Daddy sent you over to be my companion, didn't he? You might as well tag along so that you'll be earning your keep." At this malicious thrust, Audrey flushed and bit her lips.

The *Lurline* was already moving away from the pier and out to sea. Beatrice studied herself in the dressing-table mirror, pirouetting, hands on hips, her provocative face glowing with anticipation of pleasure. "There! Come along, if you're coming, Miss Chaperon!" she taunted. Then she flounced out of the stateroom, as if it were quite immaterial to her whether or not Audrey followed. The slim brunet walked slowly over to the porthole window. Beyond was the blue Pacific, and farther than the strongest telescope could see was Oahu. The sting of Beatrice's taunt swiftly waned as she drank in the view of sky and ocean stretching out before her. There was a timelessness to this beauty, and its truth did not change. She would see her home again, and it would be as if for the first time. Luka and Hanale would be there, and Luka's two brothers, who had played with her when she was a child. She turned and left the stateroom, closing the door behind her.

The sumptuously appointed Marine Veranda was

crowded with laughing, eagerly garrulous passengers, and blending with the sound of conversation and laughter were the strains of music as the native-costumed trio of musicians tuned up for the cocktail dance to celebrate departure from the mainland. Audrey looked about and saw Beatrice in her magenta frock, dancing with a tall, distinguished-looking man whose elegant sartorial appearance and aristocratic features suggested that he might be an important business executive. Head thrown back, she was laughing now at some pleasantry he had just made. At the buffet in the rear, smiling waiters in neat white jackets, black trousers, and jaunty black bow ties poured champagne or mixed cocktails for the festive guests. Now the trio began to play again, and the couples moved out onto the dance area, Beatrice with her new gallant. Audrey could not help feeling a certain wistful yearning to have someone beside her to whom she might talk, to whom she might confide thoughts and emotions rising up within her. Though she was surrounded by scores of people who savored the enjoyment of the moment, she felt as much alone as she had back in the old house on Lombard Street.

And then suddenly she started, a hand to her mouth, as she recognized a tall, black-haired man in a white flannel suit approaching the buffet, nodding to one of the waiters, and accepting a goblet of champagne. His back was to Audrey, but now he turned, and she could see him in profile.

It was the man whom she had met in The Captain's Sea Chest. The man who had walked slowly up Lombard Street to stare at the old house and then to disappear in the dark shadows of the twilight. It was the man who had introduced himself to her as Kamaki Marshall.

Chapter
FIFTEEN

THERE WAS no reason why she should feel alarm at the sight of Kamaki Marshall, Audrey told herself. When he had spoken to her in the shop on Taylor Street, her impression had been that he was a gracious, well-mannered young man with nothing mysterious about him. Yet the odd coincidence of seeing him that same evening walking along the street that led to the house in which she lived, and his stopping and looking so intently for so long a time and then disappearing, had made her wonder why he had chosen such a locale for an evening walk. And now to see him aboard ship, en route to Honolulu, made her wonder all the more what strange chance had brought their paths together.

He did not turn toward her, for at the moment when she recognized him, the purser apologetically made his way through the crowd of guests enjoying their first hospitality of the voyage and said something to him. He nodded and smiled, then went toward the exit of the beautifully decorated salon and disappeared, the purser in his wake.

Beatrice was thoroughly enjoying herself. Her distinguished-looking escort was saying something to her that made her laugh, and then she gave him an artful little smile and moved closer as they went on dancing. Audrey seated herself on one of the comfortable upholstered divans and vicariously enjoyed the music and the dancing, quite contented to watch the others. She could not help thinking about Kamaki Marshall again and wondering what motive he had had for coming to the house where she lived and what particular errand brought him aboard this ocean liner at exactly the same time she and Beatrice were sailing.

The cocktail party over at last, Beatrice walked over to her, escorted by the mature executive with whom she had danced. "Why, you poor child, didn't anyone ask you to dance?" she teased. Then, turning to her escort, she added, "This is Audrey, my cousin, Doug dear. Audrey, I want you to meet Douglas Meredith. He's a very important man in one of the biggest San Francisco advertising agencies, and he's a wonderful dancer."

"It's a pleasure to meet you, Audrey." Douglas Meredith courteously inclined his head. "You really shouldn't isolate yourself on a trip like this. One of the traditions of a Matson cruise is that everybody makes friends with everybody else, which makes the trip much more enjoyable. I myself go along with tradition, as a good many advertising men do—that's exactly why I said to myself I had to meet your very lovely red-haired cousin."

"Isn't he just adorable?" Beatrice cooed, patting Douglas Meredith's cheek with a slim, beautifully manicured forefinger. "Maybe we'll see you at dinner, Doug. Come along, Audrey, we'll want to dress in our finest for our first dinner aboard, won't we?"

Audrey's cheeks flamed at Beatrice's condescending tone, such as one would use to a recalcitrant child. "It was a pleasure to meet you, Mr. Meredith," she murmured, and meekly followed Beatrice out of the salon and back to their stateroom.

"I don't at all mind your keeping out of the way, especially when I'm with a good-looking man like that, Audrey dear," Beatrice purred as she whisked off her frock and rummaged through the wardrobe closet in search of her prettiest evening gown. She decided on an orange chiffon creation she had bought just two weeks before in preparation for the cruise. Smoothing it down over her supple body, she amusedly glanced at Audrey and remarked, "It's a pity that you didn't work long enough to earn money for a brand-new wardrobe, Audrey dear. You could certainly stand it. But then, I suppose you can always go back to wearing *muu-muus* when we get to Honolulu, can't you? Isn't that what you had on the first time you came to our house when I was a little girl?"

"Of course." Audrey tried to keep her voice from trembling with annoyance. "Almost every girl or woman on the island wears a *muu-muu,* and I'm sure it's appropriate even in the best restaurants. Mother used to tell me that the wonderful thing about Hawaii was the naturalness of it and the way people got used to being themselves and not putting on a show."

"Oh, so you think I'm showing off, do you?" Beatrice's large eyes narrowed with anger. "You're a fine one to talk. And after all Daddy's done for you, too. It wouldn't surprise me at all once you set foot on your native island, you reverted to type and went native just like the rest of the half-breeds."

"That's a vicious thing to say, Beatrice!" Audrey flashed. "If there are mixed bloods in Hawaii, it's because the white men came from the mainland and from Europe and settle there and helped build and develop the land. And they married fine girls whose blood was as good in its own right as any mainlander's. My mother was the daughter of a man who had been a chief back in Polynesia. Why should I be ashamed of her?"

"Hmph!" Beatrice sniffed, wrinkling her nose with disdain, "I'm just glad I know who my mother and father are, that's all. I wouldn't want to have any native blood in me, thank you. Well, are you coming to dinner with me?"

"Later, if you don't mind." Audrey didn't want Beatrice to see how close she was to tears of humiliation from her cousin's slander.

The red-haired beauty in the orange chiffon evening gown gave a metallic little laugh. "Suit yourself. Me, I'm going to have fun on this trip, because I earned it.

And don't forget, when we get to Honolulu, you're supposed to do what Daddy says. I don't know why he bothered to see that you get something that really ought to belong to him, after all the money he's spent and the trouble he's taken to bring you up to be a civilized person and part of our family, but the least you can do is find that deed he wants you to get. Now I'm going. See you later."

She turned this way and that, admiring her reflection in the mirror. Then, with a contemptuously sneering look at Audrey, she left the stateroom.

Audrey did not go to the dining salon that first night out; instead, ringing for the steward, she explained that she had a very bad headache and asked if he would be kind enough to bring her a tray. It was nearly midnight when Beatrice returned to the stateroom, and by then Audrey was fast asleep. She had wept a little, not out of self-pity but in distress at finding that Beatrice could still resent her and, worst of all, cast a slur upon her beloved mother. And with this anguish, too, came the sharpening premonition that Beatrice's insistence on her finding the deed to the property in Oahu must make her guard the secret of its hiding place all the more. Somehow, she sensed that it was not so much that she was a chaperon for Beatrice, but that Beatrice had been sent along with her as a guarantee that the missing deed would be found.

The theme of a night in Paris was the highlight of the second night out, prefaced by the captain's champagne party in the lounge. In the dining salon, the decor and menu emulated what a visitor to Paris might enjoy at one of the finest restaurants, and then there was a sparkling French revue given in another lounge decorated to evoke the atmosphere of a Montmartre cabaret. The weather had been ideal, and Audrey, who had decided not to lock herself up morbidly in the stateroom, had made the most of it. That afternoon she had played shuffleboard on the sundeck and watched laughing businessmen and their wives try to master the hula as native Hawaiian dancers sought to teach them the fundamentals

146

of this sensuous and evocative dance. Just before dinner, she had gone swimming in the saltwater pool. Strangely, there was no sign of Kamaki Marshall, nor did she see him at the champagne party or in the dining salon.

Beatrice seemed to ignore her now and spent much of the time during the day driving golf balls out into the sea from specially constructed greens on the afterdeck, with Douglas Meredith an attentive instructor. Or they would walk about the deck, hand in hand, gaily chatting, then pause to try a game of shuffleboard or test their marksmanship at trapshooting. Audrey did not intrude herself where they might see her, and often she spent long moments standing at the rail on the sun deck looking westward, where, on the morning of the fifth day, Oahu would appear upon the dazzling horizon of the Pacific.

The third night out was marked by a Mardi Gras festival, beginning in the cocktail lounge, which had been ingeniously decorated to suggest the French Quarter. Then there was carnival atmosphere, with hundreds of multicolored balloons soaring to the ceiling of the dining salon, where a dinner as superlative as any given at Antoine's was served. The stateroom steward that morning had smilingly informed both Audrey and Beatrice that costumes would be provided if they wished to enter the contest and the grand parade in the main ballroom after dinner. Beatrice readily agreed, and somewhat to her own surprise, Audrey decided to participate in the revelry. "May we have our choice of costumes, Steward?" Beatrice demanded.

"But of course, Miss."

"I think I'd like something with a tiger or leopard motif, if you have such a thing, Steward," the redhead declared.

"I think I might be able to find something suitable, Miss. And what might I bring you?" he turned to Audrey.

"A hula dancer's costume, if you have one, please, Steward." Audrey smiled.

147

Beatrice gave her a derisive look. "Grass skirt and all, I suppose. Didn't I say you'd go native? Only you're starting rather soon, don't you think, dear?"

"That's exactly what I'd like, Steward," Audrey interposed, ignoring her cousin's catty innuendo.

It had been a delightful evening. The black felt Venetian face mask gave Audrey the exciting security of an incognito, and she found herself chatting with others wearing the costumes of pirates, soldiers, cannibals, and fashion models, whose masks seemed to change their own personalities as much as it hid their identities. She had read about the fabulous Mardi Gras celebration, the wild revelry of the French Quarter, and the tales of romance when a girl from a prominently social family met and fell in love with a handsome masked young stranger who might on the morrow be only a grocer's clerk or a laundry-truck driver. It was exhilarating to take part in a masquerade and to forget the hateful snobbery of her cousin.

The steward had outdone himself and found an authentic hula costume. As she stared at herself in the mirror, Audrey said aloud, "I wish you could see me, Mother, after all these years, and know how much I love you to this day and how glad I am to be coming back home to you and the island where I was born."

This time, she did not sit watching others dance but joyously accepted invitations from the costumed gallants who sought her out. And the last dance was claimed by a pirate with gold earrings, a cutlass at his belt, and gleaming black boots. She thought that he was young and very handsome, and as they danced, he said to her, "You're a wonderful dancer. I knew you would be, the moment I saw you in that hula costume. One can tell, almost by instinct, that you're not a tourist, not a *malihini*."

Her eyes widened, for that voice sounded vaguely familiar in its resonance and pleasantness of tone. "I shouldn't have imagined that a bold pirate had time to learn how to dance so well," she parried.

"Oh, pirates aren't always sinking ships and making their victims walk the plank. Sometimes when there are *kona* winds and their vessels lie becalmed, they must pass the time somehow. For me, it was dancing."

"Oh, I see," Audrey laughed. A delicious, heady sensation had taken possession of her. The laughter, the gaiety, the music, and this mysterious, handsome pirate's superb command of her in guiding and leading her to the measures of the dance banished the oppressive worries about Beatrice's sudden and caustic attack against her and her very origin.

There came now the chiming of the ship's clock. "At midnight we unmask, fair lady," her pirate companion murmured. "A pirate never carries off a prize unless he knows its beauty."

"You first," Audrey teased.

"Very well." Deftly, he reached behind him and undid the strings of the mask. Audrey's fingers had gone to the strings of her own mask; now her fingers trembled and dug into her palms. For the face of the pirate was that of Kamaki Marshall.

"That's not fair," he laughed. "I've unmasked, and now it's your turn, fair lady."

"All—all right."

"We meet again," Kamaki Marshall said with a bow that would have put a Creole dandy to shame.

"Why—yes. It was in that shop on Taylor Street, wasn't it?" She tried to be nonchalant, but her heart was beating very fast. He stood so close to her, and he had held her so gently as they danced.

"That's true. And you were interested in the giant conch, as I remember."

"Yes. But I saw you again that same day."

He regarded her with a questioning expression. "Now that I don't remember."

"But that evening, you were walking up Lombard
149

Street, and you stopped in front of the house where I lived and looked at it for a long time, and then you went away," she pursued.

"I hate to contradict a beautiful lady," Kamaki Marshall smilingly replied, "but I'm sure you were mistaken. Perhaps it was someone who looked like me. I'm rather an ordinary fellow, after all. And I usually don't go walking by myself on a foggy evening in San Francisco. I'm not the bold pirate my costume suggests, you see. And it isn't the wisest thing in the world to walk by yourself at night. Besides, how could I possibly have known where you lived?"

"No, I suppose not. Perhaps it was someone who looked like you," she faltered. And yet she had been so sure. She could have sworn that it had been Kamaki Marshall whom she had seen out the dormer window. And if she were right, why had he so quickly and blandly lied to her now?

She was about to ask him why he was on this same trip with her when Beatrice's elegant voice broke in. "Why, Audrey, you little minx! Keeping this gorgeous man all to yourself and trying to pretend you wanted to stay in your stateroom all through the trip! Appearances are deceiving, I see. Isn't that the young man I saw you flirting with in that curio shop on Taylor Street?"

Audrey felt her cheeks and forehead on fire. With a gasp of shame, she turned and fled.

Chapter
SIXTEEN

CURIOUSLY ENOUGH, Beatrice Mason did not pursue her mocking disparagement of her cousin's virtue when she finally returned to the stateroom. Audrey had already undressed and gone to bed. In the morning, too, no further reference was made to the coincidence that Audrey's dancing partner had been none other than the man whom she had met at The Captain's Sea Chest. Yet the tantalizing little smile and the knowing look in her red-haired cousin's eyes told Audrey that Beatrice had not forgotten the discovery she had made the night before. Her way of proving it, Audrey discovered later that afternoon, was to meet Kamaki Marshall on deck and, linking her arm round his, lead him off to a game of shuffleboard while Audrey watched from her deck lounge chair. And at the captain's dinner and ball that marked the fourth night of the cruise, Beatrice had somehow maneuvered herself into a seat beside the handsome, black-haired young man who had shared Audrey's interest in the conch at the curio shop.

The slim brunet spent most of the last day swimming in the saltwater pool and then enjoying the sun from her lounge chair. Douglas Meredith, nattily dressed, greeted her while on a stroll around the deck that afternoon. "Good afternoon, Miss Mason. Are you enjoying the trip?"

"Yes, very much, thank you, Mr. Meredith."

He drew a morocco leather cigar case out of his coat

pocket, chose a long, slim Havana panatela, and carefully lit it. Then he cast the match over the rail and gave a rueful little chuckle. "Shipboard meetings are, alas, all too short. They don't usually last much longer than that match I just tossed over the side."

"That sounds terribly pessimistic on such a beautiful day, Mr. Meredith," Audrey replied laughingly.

"Yes, I know." He took a puff at his cigar and exhaled a series of perfect smoke rings. "But I'm sure my gloomy mood will be gone by the time we meet for Fiesta Night. The entire liner, as you can probably notice, is being transformed into the setting of Latin America with all the decorations. They tell me that even the stokers are wearing Latin American costumes instead of their dungarees."

"There's so much entertainment and so much to do, it's really a very lovely trip."

"Would you think me fickle if I invited you to have dinner with me, Miss Mason?"

"That would be very nice, thank you."

"Your cousin seems to have abandoned me for a younger man," he said wryly. "I hope that doesn't sound as if I'm making you second choice."

Audrey flushed with embarrassment. "Of course it doesn't. I'd be very glad to spend the evening with you, Mr. Meredith. Beatrice tells me you're in an advertising agency."

"If I had any ego—which your cousin has already deflated—I'd answer that I *am* the agency," he chuckled good-naturedly. "But I can't say that I blame her for picking that fellow Kamaki Marshall."

"Do you know him?" Audrey asked eagerly.

"Well, you might say we're drinking companions. He and I had a Scotch at the bar last night before turning in. He works for the City of Honolulu, in some administrative function or other. He wasn't too explicit, but I'm not the prying kind. But he's certainly remarkably sophisticated and quite a good conversationalist, even if he appears to be an islander. He did tell me that he

152

was born in Oahu, but he makes occasional trips to the mainland in connection with his work. Well, suppose I meet you right here about six o'clock in the evening. Don't forget to wear your *fiesta* costume. Not that you need any gilding of the lily to look lovely, Miss Mason."

And as he nodded and then resumed his walk around the deck, Audrey flushed again, but this time with pleasure at the suave compliment. . . .

Douglas Meredith was as able a dancer as Kamaki Marshall, Audrey discovered. There was nostalgia to this last night out, despite the gaiety of *fiesta*. Many of the passengers had made new friends and would part from them in the morning, perhaps never to see them again. For these five nights and four and a half days, everyone aboard had entered a new little world of relaxation and pleasure, and in the morning all would go their separate ways. As they finished their last dance and Douglas Meredith thanked her, Audrey saw Kamaki Marshall and Beatrice walking toward the bar. The redhead was talking animatedly with her handsome companion, and he was smiling at her. As they came up to the bar, Audrey saw Beatrice's arm familiarly curved round his waist, as if they were intimates. And an irrational impulse made her ask Douglas Meredith, "Could we take a walk around the deck for fresh air and to see the moonlight?"

He had seen her glance toward the bar, and he too had seen Beatrice and the handsome young islander. "We're even now, Miss Mason," he told Audrey, an ironic smile on his lips.

"Oh? What do you mean, Mr. Meredith?"

"Well, this afternoon when I invited you to spend the evening with me, I let it slip that you were second choice. But right now, I'd say that I was second choice for you."

Audrey gasped and blushed. "You—you're quite mistaken, Mr. Meredith. He doesn't mean a thing to me. It's just that . . . that I met him by accident in a curio shop some weeks ago, and it was just a surprise to find him aboard. I assure you it's nothing more than that."

153

"You know, your candor is most disarming, Miss Mason. Let's forget the business about second choice, shall we? I'd like very much to take you around the deck to see the ocean with the moonlight playing along its surface."

Perhaps nowhere else in the world is an arriving ship so warmly greeted as in Honolulu. A press tug and a launch went out early in the morning to meet the big white liner anchoring off Diamond Head, and the enthusiastic greeters mounted the ship's ladder saying "*Aloha*" to the passengers and garlanding them with leis. Among the greeters were lovely brown-skinned, grass-skirted Hawaiian girls who staged a hula show in the lounge as the *Lurline* proceeded majestically to its port at Aloha Tower, commandeering shy and clumsy passengers to dance the hula with them. The ship's orchestra, aided by a vocal sextet, played Hawaiian melodies, and the passengers who had crowded to the rail could see throngs milling about on the docking wharf. In the churning waters around the ship, the glistening chocolate-colored bodies of young Hawaiian divers were seen, watching for coins being tossed from the ship's decks.

As they were disembarking, Audrey saw Douglas Meredith again and thanked him for having made the last night such a pleasant one. He courteously tipped his hat. "That goes double for me, Miss Mason. Maybe I'll see you again either here or in San Francisco. By the way, if you're interested in a job at my agency when you get back, just let me know. You'll find the agency listed under my name in the phone book."

"That's very kind of you, Mr. Meredith, but you really don't know anything about me."

He looked at her steadily for a moment, then said, "I know enough already to know that you're very honest, very intelligent, and not at all a hypocrite. Those are qualities worth hiring in any business, Miss Mason. But whatever you do, I wish you good luck and every happiness."

At last the passengers of the *Lurline* said farewell to

154

the laughing and cheerful Hawaiian girls and youths who flooded around them on the dock to offer leis to those who had not already received them aboard ship, and went about the mundane business of getting to their hotels. Beatrice sank back into the back seat of the cab with a sigh of relief. "Whew! I'm glad that's over. It gets a little hectic, doesn't it?"

"Yes, but it's all so friendly."

"Oh, sure," the redhead sarcastically retorted. "All those leis and the kissing and the *alohas*, that's all part of the gimmick to make the tourists think they're big shots. It's all put on, take it from me. So this is Honolulu? Well, I'm not overly impressed. But at least I'll have somebody who knows this place to show me where there's fun to be had. Your boyfriend Kamaki Marshall. You know, that's an odd name for a man."

"Not at all, Beatrice. Kamaki means Thomas in Hawaiian. Just as my name Audrey is Aukele over here."

"Well, no matter what his name is, he's lots of fun, and he's a very important person over here, I have a notion. And he sort of goes for me. So, if you don't mind, Cousin Audrey, hands off, hm?"

Audrey started to reply, but there wasn't any need to let the cab driver overhear a private squabble. Besides, Beatrice's insinuation wasn't worthy of an answer. So she contented herself with staring out of the cab window and seeing the cosmopolitan shops and modern buildings of the capital of Hawaii. Even though her recollections from childhood of this, the largest city in the islands, were dim, she could realize what incredible expansion and development it had undergone during her absence from her birthplace.

The liveried doorman at the Royal Hawaiian ostentatiously opened the door of their cab and welcomed them to the palatial pink stucco building that dominates Waikiki Beach. A few minutes later, after a bellboy had carried their suitcases to their luxurious double room, which looked out on the ocean little more than a stone's throw away, Beatrice was again in high spirits. "This is

155

really marvelous, isn't it? Daddy was a perfect lamb to put us up here. Oh, and we'll have to go to the *luau* on Sunday out in the garden. It's very exciting and colorful, you know."

"It is beautiful," Audrey agreed, "and I'm very grateful to your father."

"Are you?" Beatrice's eyes narrowed. "Then you just remember why you're here, my meek-mannered little cousin. Just stay away from Kamaki Marshall and concentrate on finding that deed so Daddy won't have any trouble when he has to go to court on your behalf in October."

"Beatrice, I'm not exactly a child, and your father already told me that he'd like me to find it. You don't have to keep needling me about it."

"Ha!" Beatrice uttered a strident little laugh. "What's really needling you is that I've taken over your boyfriend, that's what. Anyway, he's a real man, not one of those half-breeds like the kind we saw diving for quarters and dimes at the dock."

"And again you keep reminding me that my mother came from this island," Audrey spiritedly countered. "I told you I don't have the same outlook that you do. And I'd advise you, while you're a guest of the island, not to let anyone else except myself hear you talking about half-breeds. That's an insult. If you want to go back into genealogy, you'll find that the pureblooded Hawaiian had a very old culture long before America was even discovered. But that's not important. What really matters is that everyone who came to this island in search of freedom or health or work discovered tolerance and understanding. That's what *aloha* really means, Beatrice. Love and understanding of all people."

"Please don't try to give me a lecture on Hawaiian customs," Beatrice snapped as she began to unpack her suitcases. "I'm here to have fun, not to settle down and become a Hawaiian, I assure you." Then, with a malicious glance at the slim brunet, she added, "Unless, of

156

course, Kamaki Marshall gets so interesting that I might be persuaded to stay here with him."

Audrey wordlessly began to unpack her own suitcase, while Beatrice changed into a summery short-sleeved blue cotton dress. "I'm going to lunch, and then I think I'll do some sightseeing," she announced.

"You go ahead," Audrey answered. "I want to visit Aunt Luka and see the house where I was born."

"Oh, that's right. Well, I wouldn't want to intrude on such a sentimental reunion," the redhead laughed. "Maybe I'll meet Kamaki Marshall and have dinner with him. So I'll see you when I see you."

She closed the door of the luxurious room behind her, and a few moments later the liveried doorman telephoned for a cab to be sent to the entrance of the Royal Hawaiian. Beatrice impatiently waited, tapping her foot with nervous irritability, till at last the cab drew up and the doorman deferentially opened the door for her to enter.

Opening her purse, she took out the envelope her father had given her, swiftly opened it, and glanced at the letter. Then she said to the driver, "I want to go to two sixty nine and a half Lewers Road. And I'm in a hurry!"

157

Chapter
SEVENTEEN

AN HOUR LATER, Audrey Mason stepped into a cab and gave the driver the address of the house on Waimanalo Beach. She had changed into a red-and-green *muu-muu* and thong sandals, and she still wore the plumeria lei an admiringly grinning Hawaiian youth had put about her neck during the ceremony of docking at the Aloha Tower. Alone now and with only a few minutes between her and this first visit to the house with the spired weather vane and the magnificent garden, she could even put out of her mind Beatrice's malignant reference to Milliama's race, though she would not soon forgive her cousin for that unpardonable insult.

She had wanted to write Luka that she was coming, but Uncle Dan had told her that he would wire ahead. It was strange that Luka and Hanale hadn't been at the dock to meet her. But that didn't matter. She knew that Hanale still worked in the pineapple fields of Ewa; perhaps he hadn't been able to get off work and to bring Luka. It didn't matter. She would see them again. She wondered how much they had changed. More than ever, after what Beatrice had said about "islanders," she wanted to be with them again and to remember the happy times of her childhood. The warm, sunny day and the sight of the palm trees and the colorfully casual costumes even of the tourists on Kalakua Avenue were a glorious deliverance from the broodingly silent and gloomy house on Lombard Street.

"Will you be coming back, Miss? I can wait, if you like," the driver offered. But Audrey shook her head. "No, thank you. I'm going to visit some very dear friends whom I haven't seen in many years. Here you are."

"*Mahalo a nui loa*," the driver said as she paid him.

"Doesn't that mean 'Thank you very much'?" Audrey laughed as she got out of the cab.

"*Pololei!*" The driver chuckled. "You are not a *malihini*, I know. I think you come back home."

"Yes, that's true," Audrey murmured softly, strangely moved by the taxi driver's perception. "But it's been so long ago that I've almost forgotten."

The driver shook his head. "You don't forget the island once you've been here. It gets in your blood. Well, good luck and *a hui hou kaua*." He waved his hand and then drove back to town along the paved road. And once again Audrey was moved, for his farewell greeting to her had been exactly that which Luka had uttered nearly fourteen years ago.

How beautiful the garden was, as if it had been tended all this while by a loving hand! It was even more breathtaking than she remembered it, when her mother had taken her for walks along the narrow winding path. There were the proud flame flowers of the orange trumpet vine, and the cream and rose blossoms of the oleander, growing in extravagant abundance upon their tall shrubs and set off by the slender, pointed dull-green leaves. She breathed in the cloyingly sweet scent of *pikake*, the little white ten-petaled flower named after the peacock that was beloved by Princess Kaiulani, that beautiful daughter of Hawaii's last king, who lived in Manoa Valley and whom Robert Louis Stevenson so much admired.

Audrey drank in the perfume and the beauty of these lavish flowers, growing side by side, so different and yet so harmonious in their decorative unison. Yes, they lived side by side, flourishing and sturdy, renewing their beauty with each new year. They were like the peoples of Hawaii themselves, and they showed how many different races could come together and live harmoniously side by side. In this garden, Audrey thought, were the allegorical refutations of Beatrice's contempt for the "half-breed."

And here were the steps and the veranda and the house. And there were the beach on which she had played with her mother and the blue ocean into whose gently lapping little waves breaking upon the shore she had first ventured so many years ago. There was a stillness and a peace to this enchanted place, and it was hers because it had been her parents'. Luka had often told her that the good spirits whom Kalaiki had summoned when the house was built would guard the spirits of her father and mother so that they might always be within this house to bless it and to bless her for all the days of her life.

The door was open, as if in welcome to her. And as she ascended the steps and walked on the veranda towards it, matronly Luka, uttering a cry of incredulous joy, came out to meet her and hugged and kissed her as if she were still that same little child of long ago.

"Aukele!" she exclaimed, and there were tears in her eyes. "I knew that your *hoku* would bring you back to us, *hiwahiwa*. How grown you are, a woman already, and yes, even more beautiful than Milliama!"

"Luka, Luka, it's so good to be back! But didn't you know I was coming? Uncle Dan said that he was going to wire you."

Luka shook her head. "No, Aukele, I had no word from the mainland that you were coming. Only a few hours ago I learned of it through my very good friend. He is here, Aukele. Come meet him."

She took Audrey by the hand just as she had done in the past and led the slim brunet across the threshold of the house in which Philip and Milliama Mason had know those all too short years of perfect happiness. And there, standing before the fireplace, smiling, was Kamaki Marshall.

"We've already met, Luka," he explained to the hand-

161

some Hawaiian matron, who was dabbing at her tear-filled eyes and smiling at them both.

"You—you know him, Luka?" Audrey stammered.

"But of course, my dear one. He has come to this house many times the last few years to keep it in order for the day of your return. He is a good friend, and you can trust him, *hiwahiwa*."

"But I don't understand, Luka. Mr. Marshall, all I know is that I met you in that curio shop and then just now you were on the *Lurline*."

"I do owe you an explanation, Miss Mason. You see, my father, who came from England many years ago, lived in a house near Lanikai, just beyond where Bellows Field now is. He married a girl from Papeete, and he knew Luka's father and your grandfather, Kalaiki. I knew your father, too, you see."

"You knew my father? Tell me what he was like, please, Mr. Marshall. I was only a baby when he was killed on Pearl Harbor Day, and I don't remember him at all, only from what my mother used to tell me."

"I was only a little boy then of about six or seven," Kamaki Marshall replied, "but my father had told me what a fine teacher he was and how the children loved him. I think it was hearing this and meeting him and talking with him and understanding the love he had for this island and its people that made me decide to become a schoolteacher myself. I teach at Punaluu, Miss Mason. I've had sabbatical leave since last fall because I'm going to take an advanced degree and write a thesis on the history of education in Hawaii. That was why you saw me in San Francisco. I have some dear friends there who went to the University of Hawaii with me, and I was visiting them."

"Thank you for what you said about my father, Mr. Marshall. That's what my mother told me, but it's good to know that a stranger knew and liked my father. And then, too, I must confess I was a little suspicious of you. It was so strange that I met you first at the shop, and then you turned up on the *Lurline*. But tell me the truth—

was I wrong in thinking that you were the man who walked along Lombard Street and stood looking at the house that same evening?"

He turned toward her and stood facing her, his face very grave. "No, you were right. I'm sorry if I seemed to mislead you. Luka had asked me to go by the house and to see how you were, to see where you lived on the mainland. I thought even of ringing the bell and asking to see you but decided against it. I thought it might upset you. That's why I stood so long looking, making up my mind whether I should go in or not."

"That all makes it so very clear, Mr. Marshall," Audrey laughed. "I'm very glad you told me. I was beginning to conjure up all sorts of mysterious things about you." Then, with that instinct which all women have, she teased, "And of course, you were so wrapped up in Beatrice that I thought you didn't like me at all."

"That's not true at all, Miss Mason. Luka wanted me to try to meet your cousin when I was in San Francisco. But it was just by chance that the two of you and I had the same sailing date."

"That *is* a relief to know, Mr. Marshall. I thought maybe you were following me. Then, of course, when you spent all that time with Beatrice, I was just a little hurt, I'll admit."

"I would never want to hurt you. Luka has told me that this house and land belong to you. And she has told me, too, that she made you promise to keep the secret of the conch shell. But that was all she said; she did not tell me what the secret was."

Audrey gasped, turning to Luka for verification. The handsome matron nodded. "Yes, *hiwahiwa*, that is true. Kamaki Marshall is an islander as you are, Aukele. And for many years he has been a friend to Hanale and me. Why, even now he is teaching the children of Keoki and Kelolo. He is one of us, *hiwahiwa*. But I have worried that away from the island all these years, you might forget your birthright and others might wish to take it from you."

"Luka, I'll be twenty-one in October, and at that time I'll inherit what my father and mother left to me. But Uncle Dan sent me over with his daughter to be her companion, and he told me that he needs the deed so that when I come of age there will be no difficulty in claiming my inheritance."

"I do not know what the laws are, *hiwahiwa*, but it seems to me that when my father sold this land to your father, the sale was written down in the landbooks which they keep in Honolulu. Is that not true, Kamaki?"

"Yes, that's true enough, Luka. On Monday I'll take Miss Mason to the Bureau of Conveyances, and we'll look up what it says in the book just so there can be no difficulties for her."

"That's very kind of you, Mr. Marshall. Of course, I'll have to turn over the deed to prove my right when I come of age."

"One of my good friends in Honolulu is a lawyer, and I'm sure he would be happy to represent you, Miss Mason, when the right time comes to produce the deed. Perhaps you'd like to meet him Monday."

"Yes, it would probably be a good idea, Mr. Marshall. Luka, may I stay and see Hanale and your brothers?"

Luka laughed happily as she embraced the slim brunet. "I should be very angry with you if you did not, *hiwahiwa*. You and Kamaki Marshall will be my guests at a special *luau* at my house this evening."

Chapter
EIGHTEEN

THAT EVENING was a joyous one for Audrey, and the pleasant little *luau* in the garden of the house of Hanale and Luka had the warmth and comradeship most appropriate to her return to her homeland. She played with the children of Keoki and Kelolo, and yet she was careful not to devote all her attention to them, knowing the hidden sorrow Luka and Hanale had over their childlessness. Kamaki Marshall, speaking fluent Hawaiian, helped her remember many of the picturesquely descriptive phrases she had learned and then forgotten through disuse. Altogether, it was a welcome diametrically opposed to the one that Dan Mason's children had given her that dark November evening nearly fourteen years ago.

It was well past eleven that night when she reluctantly said her goodbyes to Luka and Hanale and to Luka's brothers' wives and children. Kamaki Marshall drove her back to the Royal Hawaiian in his own old Chevy. "On Monday, Aukele," he said to her as the doorman helped her out of the car, "I'll call for you and take you to the Bureau of Conveyances."

"Thanks so much, Mr. Marshall. I—I owe you an apology for having mistrusted you."

"Well," he said with a boyish grin. "the best apology you could make is to stop calling me 'Mr. Marshall.' I'm not so much older than you, after all, just twenty-eight, and I'd like you to call me Kamaki."

"It's a promise, then, Kamaki," she called to him with delighted laughter in her voice as the doorman ostentatiously held open the door of the entrance. And she saw him wave and nod with another disarming grin as he started up the Chevy and drove out along the winding paved road flanked by rolling green lawns and towering palm trees.

Beatrice was in negligee, finishing a letter, as she entered. "Well, you had a time for yourself, didn't you?" the redhead greeted her. "It must have been a scene out of *East Lynne*. I had lots more fun. Douglas Meredith gave me a ring and took me to dinner at Canlis' Charcoal Broiler. What a beautiful restaurant, and what wonderful steaks and shrimp cocktail we had! I haven't had better even at the best places in San Francisco. And tomorrow he's taking me to The Willows. That's where they have that dining room right in a tropical park, and the terrace where you eat is over a big pond where the carp and the crabs and the ducks fight for the crumbs you throw them. And after that Doug says he's going to take me to some of the night spots even the tourists don't get to see."

"I'm glad you're having such a good time, Beatrice."

"Thanks for nothing. Oh, by the way, when you were back at that house of yours, did you look for the deed the way Daddy wanted you to?"

"Not yet, Beatrice. We're going to be here for a few weeks, aren't we? I certainly wasn't going to do it the very first day. And I spent the evening with my mother's half-sister and her husband and her brothers and their children. It wasn't a time to think about being greedy."

"You're such a goody-goody, Audrey, but I don't consider looking after your own interests being greedy. If I'd been you, I'd have found that deed right away just to make sure of everything."

"That's where we're different, Beatrice. Good night."

Audrey spent Saturday visiting the International Market Place and windowshopping along Kalakaua Avenue. On Sunday, which was the Fourth of July, she and Beatrice attended the gala *luau* held in the garden of the Royal Hawaiian overlooking Waikiki Beach. Beatrice, openly sniffing at Audrey's *muu-muu*, dressed in one of her smartest frocks, and when they were seated at one of the tables near the stage, she whispered loud enough for others to hear, "Boy, is this corny!"

Audrey did not answer, for at that moment the Master of the Feast, dressed in the feather headdress of a Hawaiian chief, stepped out upon the stage, lifted a huge conch shell to his lips, and blew the summons to the *luau*. And vividly she remembered the secret Luka had confided. Yes, she knew that the deed to her father's land and house was hidden in the conch shell under a papaya tree in the garden. Now that she was sure of her secret, now that she had an ally in the mysterious young stranger, she need not worry about the future. Not even Beatrice's hostility could hurt her.

After the feast, which Beatrice superciliously criticized as "primitive food, and they want a fantastic price for it," there was dancing. First by the *Tutus*, the grandmothers who did their quaint versions of the stately hula to the plaudits of the cheerful crowd who thronged the garden. Then the traditional dances by the finest dancers on the island, and finally the thrilling Samoan fire dance by a handsome young Samoan prince. The moon was full, and the stars sparkled in the sky. It was wonderfully new to Audrey; yet with each passing moment she felt herself less a stranger. "I've come home at last," she murmured to herself as she walked back to the elevator while Beatrice went over to the desk to mail a letter she had written earlier that day. . . .

The little Chinese clerk in the office of the Bureau of Conveyances wished Kamaki Marshall and Audrey Mason a good morning and inquired how he could serve them. Audrey explained, "My father had a house and some land on Waimanalo Beach. As I'm the only living heir and will come of age in October, I came here today

167

to ask if you would look up in your records the title of this land."

"I see. You have the original deed to the land, Miss Mason?"

Audrey gave Kamaki Marshall a quick, appealing look. He nodded. "I know where to find it," she explained.

"Do you have the description or the correct location of this property?" the little clerk inquired.

After Audrey had given him the information, he bowed low and asked her to wait a few moments till he could locate the ledger. He would have to go back to the books of 1938 and 1939, and they were kept in a special vault. Audrey thanked him, and she and Kamaki Marshall sat down on the bench near the door of the office. "I can hardly believe that I'm home at last, Kamaki," she said shyly.

"Do you plan to stay here or to go back to San Francisco?"

"I really don't know. I have a job to go back to, and I owe my employers a certain loyalty, because they've been very good to me. I hadn't even worked there long enough to deserve this vacation, as it is."

"Loyalty and honor mean much to you, Aukele. Just as they did to your father and to your mother."

"Thank you, Kamaki. Did you know my mother, too?"

He nodded with a gentle smile. "Someday I will tell you many things about your parents. But you must trust me. I know that it seems strange to you that I'm meddling in your affairs, but it was Luka's wish. She loves you as much as she would love her own child. That's why she wanted me to help."

"I—I'd never say that you were meddling, Kamaki. You've been very kind. Yet in a way, I owe Uncle Dan so very much for all he's done. I've been wondering if I shouldn't let him have the property so that he could sell it and take out of the sale what I've owed him for my keep."

"You are talking like a mainlander, Aukele. Here we

don't put a value of dollars and cents on hospitality. I know a family in Manoa that has very little money, but they brought up as their own child a Chinese baby that was abandoned by its parents. That baby is in my classroom now at Punaluu, and when he grows to manhood, they will not ask him to pay them back for every bowl of rice or every pair of sandals. Your father and mother meant the house and land for you. And besides, you have given this Dan Mason as much as you have taken. You have given him understanding and kindness and gentleness, like one of his own children." She blushed at his words and was about to speak, when the little clerk came back to the counter, his face grave with concern.

"I think I have found the tract of which you speak, Miss Mason," he said as he spread open the huge ledger to the place he had already marked with a sheet of foolscap. "Here it is, the acre of land off Waimanalo Beach, sold by Kalaiki to one Philip Mason."

"Yes, that's it!" Audrey exclaimed.

"Then you are the daughter of Philip Mason?"

"That is true."

"Unfortunately, Miss Mason, there is a further entry in this ledger which calls attention to a subsequent transaction made in the spring of nineteen forty-one. I will have to consult that volume too, if you will be kind enough to wait."

"Certainly. And thank you so much for all your trouble."

Audrey turned to Kamaki Marshall, her eyes questioning. "A further entry? I don't understand, Kamaki."

"I don't either. We'll have to wait until he finds the ledger."

Five minutes later the little clerk, staggering under the weight of the heavy ledger, laid it atop the counter and once again spread it open to a place marked with a sheet of paper. "I have found another transaction recorded in this later book of records, Miss Mason. There is a recording here of a quitclaim deed, effected March twelve, nineteen forty-one by which your father deeded

169

the property in turn to one Dan Mason of San Francisco. This would mean that Dan Mason now owns the house and land on Waimanalo Beach. You did not know about this?"

Audrey stared helplessly at Kamaki Marshall, then shook her head. "No, I knew nothing at all about it. All my mother ever told me was that one day I should grow up to live in that house on the beach. And Luka—her half-sister—told me this before I went to San Francisco to live with this Dan Mason, who was my father's cousin. I don't understand this."

"I am very sorry to give you such bad news, Miss Mason. Of course, it is possible that there are other records, though there is no other cross-reference to this particular tract you say you are to inherit. And it would be necessary to have the original documents showing the deed and the quitclaim deed. Possibly these should be taken to the court. But this is all that I can do for you, I am afraid."

"Thank you for all your trouble," Kamaki Marshall interposed. "Aukele, I think the time has come for you to tell me your secret and to let me be your true friend."

He took her hand as they walked down the stairs to the street. "What does it all mean, Kamaki?" she asked again. "And if Uncle Dan really does own the land after all, why did he keep asking me to find the original deed?"

"I don't know, Aukele. But we are going to find out the truth. Count on me. And one thing more . . ."

"Yes, Kamaki?" She turned to him with anxiously questioning gaze.

"You must trust me. If I seem to do things you don't understand, have no fear. This is all I ask, Aukele."

"I'll trust you, Kamaki. You don't have to ask that. If you knew my father and mother as a little boy, and you are a schoolteacher as my father was, you've no need to ask."

"We've looked all through the house, señor Aguinaldo!" Beatrice exclaimed impatiently. "There's not a single sign of any deed."

170

The bespectacled little Filipino realtor whom Dan Mason had met at the Queen's Surf drew out a handkerchief and mopped his brow. "Patience, señorita Mason. My guess is that it is hidden somewhere, perhaps even buried out there in the garden. And I am convinced that your cousin knows the secret. Either her mother or that woman Luka must have told her when she was a child."

"We've got to find it so that we can substitute this quitclaim deed."

"The copy of the quitclaim deed," the Filipino realtor corrected with a knowing smile. "My friend who is a trusted clerk in the Bureau of Conveyances has already made the entries in the tract ledgers. This means that your father is shown as the present owner of this property. And another dear friend of mine, who is a handwriting expert and who has never yet been in trouble, shall we say, made both of the documents I refer to. I myself have the so-called original that shows that Philip Mason conveyed the land and the house to your father in the spring of nineteen forty-one. And by the way, when you telephone your father that I have taken care of my part of the bargain, you will tell him that the money he sent was a sufficient first payment, but my friends and I will expect another soon. And then, of course, when the property is sold, there will be a final settlement."

"I don't care to know about any arrangements you have with my father. I'm simply doing what my father wished me to do, Señor Aguinaldo," the redhead retorted. "And I won't be satisfied that you've done your part until we can find the original deed. You know perfectly well that if my cousin finds the original paper, even your skillful forgeries won't hold up in court. There'll be investigations."

"I know my business, señorita Mason, and it would be wiser if instead of threatening me you cooperated." The little Filipino drew himself up with pretentious dignity. "I can go no further than I have already gone. It is up to you to learn from your cousin where that original deed is hidden. And then you must return it to your father so that he will have all the documents necessary to claim the property."

"I think my cousin may visit the house very soon," Beatrice replied. "I shouldn't be surprised if she tried to find the deed by herself when no one's around. I'll wait here, and you go back to town. I'll call you as soon as I find out anything."

"As you say, señorita Mason. I will expect to hear from you." He turned on his heel and left the house. Beatrice Mason watched him leave, a contemptuous smile on her elegantly lovely face. Then she walked out onto the veranda and looked out over the beach and the blue ocean. "It's such a beautiful place," she said aloud, "and it's much too good for that sneaky little half-breed. Besides, Daddy'll be doing her a favor. He's a businessman, and he'll be able to get a lot of money for this place, and he'll give her enough to live like a native here on this island. And we'll be rich again the way we always should have been." She lit a cigarette and savored it, flicking ashes with an imperious hand as she walked along the veranda, like a patrician who takes stock of her possesssions. Then she went down the stairs and out into the garden, walking slowly down the winding path, admiring the perfumed fragrance of this multitude of tropical blossoms.

A car was coming down the road, and slowing now. She crouched, so that she could not be seen, then made her way along the fence till she found a hiding place amid a huge clump of oleanders. The car had stopped now, and a girl and a man were getting out—it was Audrey and Kamaki Marshall. Her intuition had been perfect. Of course the little fool knew where the deed was hidden. And if she held her breath and was very, very still, and if they came out here into the garden and talked, she might learn the secret that would give her the rightful place in San Francisco society she deserved because of her mother's own place. And with money, that place would be easier to gain. But why was Kamaki Marshall taking any interest in that meek little goodygoody? He was a fascinating man, and she had found him wonderful company. Well, money talked, and when she became the heiress, he'd be wise enough to prefer her to Audrey. Besides, she was prettier than Audrey, and she knew how to dress. That silly *muu-muu*, just like a native girl!

The little gate creaked open, and Audrey and Kamaki Marshall came down the path. Beatrice could overhear her cousin's words. "I still don't understand, Kamaki, why Uncle Dan made such a point of my looking for the deed if my father actually did sell him the land. And why didn't Luka know about that?"

"These are things I can't answer, Aukele. You must tell me if you know where this paper is hidden. It will prove your right to the land and the house. And then we must find the other paper, if it really exists."

"Kamaki! Do you mean that maybe it isn't true, after all? But the clerk at the Bureau of Conveyances said that there was a later entry showing that my father had sold the land to Uncle Dan."

"I know this, Aukele. But just the same, nothing can be done until we understand everything that has happened. And the first step is to find the paper your father had from Kalaiki. You said that you would trust me. I ask you now to tell me where it is hidden, if you can remember."

"Yes, I do remember. Luka said that my father buried it in a conch shell under the great papaya tree in the garden."

"Then we shall dig there and find it." They walked past the shrubs behind which Beatrice was hiding and on toward the still distant back of the house with the spired weathervane. Her eyes glowing with triumph, the red-haired daughter of Dan Mason crept along the ground till she had reached the little iron gate that led to the sumptuous and verdant garden. Then, stealthily opening the gate, she banged it shut, went back into the garden, and called out, "Audrey! Audrey, are you here?"

Audrey and Kamaki Marshall were standing within the circular clearing marked off by the five papaya trees.

173

"It's Beatrice," Audrey gasped. "I wonder what she wants and why she thought of looking for me here."

"Let's find out."

"Well, what a nice surprise! Kamaki, what are you doing here?" Beatrice exclaimed airily as the two came up toward her on the walk.

"I met your cousin in town, and she asked if I would drive her back to the house in which she was born," Kamaki Marshall calmly explained.

"Isn't he a darling, Audrey?" Beatrice giggled. "But you know, Audrey, you're supposed to be my companion on this trip. Poor old Doug had to go back to his stuffy advertising agency in San Francisco this morning, so I haven't anyone at all to show me the sights."

"What would you like to see, Beatrice?" Audrey pleasantly asked.

"Well, a bus ride round the island, for one thing, would be nice. And then, you remember, Audrey, how much fun we had down in Santa Cruz learning how to surf? I'm told Hawaii is the place for surfing, and I'd love to see how much I remember of what Sue Wells's husband taught me. How about you?"

"That sounds very nice, Beatrice. Kamaki, would you like to come along with us on the bus? In a way, I'm just as much a *malihini* as Beatrice is, though it must be pretty dull to you."

"I'll drive you both back, and we'll get a bite of lunch, but as a *kamaaina*, I absolutely refuse to let you take a tourist bus. I'll drive you both around myself," Kamaki replied.

Chapter
NINETEEN

KAMAKI MARSHALL had driven Audrey and Beatrice back to the Royal Hawaiian Hotel, where they had had sandwiches and iced tea, then waited in the lobby while Beatrice inquired about the renting of surfboards. He had told her that a drive around the windward side of Oahu would take most of the afternoon, but the redhead had proposed that they drive only for about three or four hours and then go back to the beach for surfing just before twilight. "It'll give us a wonderful appetite for dinner," she had explained.

Audrey came to sit down beside him on the divan in the lobby while they waited. She was frankly puzzled, and she told Kamaki Marshall as much.

"I wonder why she's so friendly all of a sudden, Kamaki," she said. "And it's strange that she came to find me just the time when we were going to look for the deed."

"I've been thinking that too, Aukele. Have you ever heard how they hunt the tiger in Africa?"

She shook her head, an uncomprehending look on her lovely face.

"Sometimes when a village is threatened by a man-eating tiger, the warriors of the village tether a goat in a little clearing well beyond their huts. And they set a trap covered over with bushes and earth so that when the tiger comes for his prey, he will fall into the trap. I think your cousin would understand that story even bet-

175

ter than you, gentle Aukele, for you do not believe in evil, and you do not believe that anyone would wish to harm you."

"Are you trying to say that Beatrice knows something about this deed and the one my father made to give Uncle Dan the house and the land on Waimanalo Beach, Kamaki?"

"I am saying only that you and I will see what will happen when it is time for us to see. You have promised to trust me. Ah, there she comes now."

"I'm ready. They say we can pick up the boards when we come back and take them out until tomorrow," Beatrice called gaily as she walked up to the divan. "Now then, Kamaki, let's go see the sights you promised to show me."

Even Beatrice, jaded as she was, could not help expressing grudging admiration for the scenic glories on the road along which Kamaki Marshall drove. Past Waimanalo Beach and on around Beach Park through Kaneohe Bay, where Kamaki Marshall pointed out the little frame house in which he lived. Then back to Koko Head and the famous blowhole where the sea is forced through a tiny hole in a lava ledge and spurts miniature geysers high into the air.

"I must admit it's gorgeous." Beatrice lit a cigarette. "Of course, that geyser can't hold a candle to Old Faithful, but I suppose the Hawaiians have to have something to boast about. But what's the really most breathtaking view you've got on this island, Kamaki?"

"The view from Nuuanu Pali," the young schoolteacher at once replied. "But if you intend to do any surfing before it gets dark, it'll have to be a quick trip."

"Oh, we'll be here several weeks, and there's plenty of time to go back and catch up on what we've missed, Kamaki dear," Beatrice cooed as she snuggled closer to him in the front seat of the Chevy. Audrey, beside her, felt again an unreasonable twinge of annoyance at this proprietary attitude. She had been silent most of the drive, for the view had enthralled her. She had been much too young to remember all the landmarks of this unsurpassable scenery; yet as the car sped along the paved road, around the bays and the green fields, with the ocean always just beyond in all its limitless majesty, she had felt that this in truth was where she belonged. And somehow, it didn't matter about the house and the land on Waimanalo Beach. Perhaps her father had had financial setbacks—perhaps her mother had been very sick and he had had to sell the house to Uncle Dan to get money so that her mother and she might not be in want. Well, let him have it, then, and she would owe him nothing for his guardianship all these years. Surely there was some work she could find on this beautiful island that had been her birthplace.

The road was steep, but it was new, and at the base of the majestic cliffs of the Pali there pierced the arterial tunnels that made way for the automobiles onto roads that led to both leeward and windward sides of Oahu. Where the spears of the warriors of King Kalanikupule had failed to defeat their foe, modern engineering had won. Yet those tunnels, even in their modern context, seemed to magnify the towering grandeur of this peak of the Koolau Mountains. These mountains rose gradually on the lee side of Oahu to nearly two thousand feet, only to drop back in one glorious plunge to the windward land sloping down to Kaneohe. Here was the ridge, nature's own knife edge mile after mile. And the Pali itself was like a vast green wall. Kamaki Marshall parked the car at the paved shoulder of the scenic road, and the three of them got out and walked over toward the rail that circled the parapet of the highway, sculptured from the very rock itself.

"Oh, how magnificent!" Audrey breathed, rapt with wonder. Beyond her and to windward, she could see the buildings of Honolulu and then the merging blue of ocean and sky. Down below, in the valley, the clear air and the towering cliff made the tiny houses seem within walking distance. And over to the right just slightly stretched the brilliant green wands decorated with tiny strips of sand, the grounds of the Pali Golf Course just to the left of Mount Olomana.

It was nearly four o'clock, and the wind was beginning to rush from the leeward side of the island down into the funnel-like gap the Pali guarded. Here the great battle which King Kamehameha had won to unify Hawaii had been staged in one of the world's most exciting geological wonders.

"I'll admit this is quite a sight," Beatrice agreed. "I wish I'd brought a camera with me. Oh, look down there, Audrey! What a lovely bunch of flowers growing just beyond the rail. One could almost reach out and pick them."

"If one were a mountain goat, yes, one could," Kamaki Marshall soberly interposed. "But there happens to be a straight drop of about five hundred feet, and I wouldn't risk it for the sake of a few flowers, beautiful though they are."

He was standing just behind Beatrice and a little to her left, and now he glanced up at the sky. "We'd best be getting back for our surfing. At that, the water may be a bit rough this time of afternoon."

"Oh, what an idiot I am!" Beatrice exclaimed. "I did bring a camera after all. I got it at the hotel camera shop and then I forgot all about it. Go get it for me, that's a dear, Kamaki."

"All right." He turned back to the car, then stopped and looked back. Beatrice seemed closer now to Audrey, and there was a cigarette in her right hand, which was lowered at her side. Now the hand was rising slowly. "Aukele, come here," he called. The slim brunet turned, as did Beatrice, her face an impassive mask, the cigarette now between her lips. Audrey walked forward towards him. "Yes, Kamaki?"

"Where shall we surf this afternoon? Certainly not Makaha."

"Oh no, I'm not good enough for that. But my mother

178

said that there was good surfing at Makapuu Point. Perhaps we could try there."

He opened the door and saw a camera on the back seat. A moment later, he brought it back to Beatrice. "No wonder I didn't see it, you'd left it in the back seat. Well, go ahead and take your pictures, but hurry. Don't you think we ought to put the surfing off until tomorrow? Makapuu Point might be rough, judging from that tradewind."

"Well, of course, if you and Audrey are afraid," Beatrice drawled as she crushed out her cigarette under her heel, "we can go down to Waikiki Beach and use paddleboards. But I like excitement. And all you've shown me so far is a lot of hills and valleys and bays and flowers. Oh, they're beautiful, sure. But I'm afraid I'd get bored if I had to live here the year round. There's too much of a sameness." She adjusted the camera and flicked the shutter. "There. One's enough. I'll take it along tomorrow when we have more time. Let's go back. I want to beat both of you—or isn't surfing one of your many accomplishments, Kamaki?"

"I've done a little, yes. I think I can keep up with you. Only I wouldn't go out too far off Makapuu Point. There are reefs there."

"I'll have you know I was on the swimming team in school," Beatrice laughed as she got into the car. "So was Audrey. So we're going to defend the honor of the mainland against you, Kamaki."

It was only a few miles from Philip Mason's house to Makapuu Point, and it was just a little before five o'clock when Kamaki Marshall parked the Chevy off the road. The water here was a darker blue, and several miles beyond the Point one could see the almost black stretch below which lurked the coral reefs. The tradewind was brisk, and the point of land jutting out into the Pacific made the incoming swells refract so that the waves swept in for a considerable distance before breaking.

179

"Well, what do you think, Kamaki?" Audrey laughed as she got out of the car and stood beside him. They had changed into their swimsuits back at the hotel—Kamaki himself had gone into the beachhouse to put on his trunks—and they had brought along the fast-turning Malibu boards. Kamaki had explained that these boards made riding shorebreak possible, so that surfers could easily take off in a fast-collapsing wave, get a short, swift ride, and then pull out before the wave closed over them.

"Frankly, I'd rather try it early in the morning," he answered as he stared out to sea. "This wind is changing and getting stronger, and I shouldn't be surprised if you'd have gutter rip out there."

"What in the world is a gutter rip?" Beatrice drew her bathing cap over her coronet braid and smoothed the bright yellow rubber down before fastening the snaps under her throat.

"Well, this point is making the waves come farther in to shore. But there's a lot of small valleylike depressions in the sand along the water's edge. So when the surf comes up on the beach, it drains into those depressions at the same time that it retreats back out into the ocean. When the water's sweeping down through those gutters, it's very fast. I'm sure your mother would never have let you go out very far off this spot, Aukele."

"Well, we're not children now," Beatrice admonished. Lifting her surfboard, she strode confidently to the water's edge, glancing back to call, "I'll treat you all to dinner at Michel's if I'm not the best surfer around these parts!"

Kamaki turned to Audrey, an exquisite figure in her blue bathing suit. A white cap covered her thick black curls and intensified the pure cameo of her face. "Be careful, Aukele."

"It's really no worse than it was at Santa Cruz, Kamaki. But I won't go out too far."

"I won't either. Those gutter rips might carry you way out to the reefs, and even a good swimmer stays away from sharp coral," he warned.

180

Beatrice had launched her board and was paddling out in the prone position, her head up, using swift overarm strokes that drove her smoothly toward the waves. They were smooth-rolling and steady now, with no hint of danger. Judging her time, she came to her feet, saw the white water starting off to her left, and dug in with a final strong pull. The swell came, the nose of her board tipped down, and she balanced in that breathtaking symmetry of one swimmer against surging ocean.

"She's very good," Kamaki Marshall pronounced. "All right, let's try our skill, shall we, Aukele?"

Once again Audrey relived the joy she had first learned during that summer at Santa Cruz. The waves were higher now, and breaking more sharply, and their challenge was exhilarating. Kamaki, bronzed and gleaming aloft on his board, smiled at her as they rode the crest of a wave side by side to its finish.

But Beatrice was paddling out farther, to catch the larger waves. "She's trying to show off," Kamaki said, shaking his head. "Well, so far the water hasn't given us any trouble. Let's get out there."

The redhead had reached nearly out to where the dark blue water blackened to herald the dangerous reefs. Laughing and waving as she lay prone on the board awaiting her chance, she beckoned to them. Audrey paddled swiftly forward, Kamaki just behind her. Suddenly a jagged, unexpected wave lifted in front of Audrey, and she turned turtle, holding on to her board and going under for safety. When she emerged, she saw a large wave roll in toward her with Beatrice aloft, balancing with left foot forward, leaning forward. Kamaki lifted his head and saw the sharp head of Beatrice's board turn ever so slightly as the redhead imperceptibly shifted her body. He dived and, catching Audrey's board, turned it turtle again, pulling her under with him just as Beatrice's board shot over them.

"That was much too close for comfort," he gasped when they came to the surface. "Let's call it quits for today."

But at that moment, a strident cry of terror rose. The wave had broken short, tumbling Beatrice off her board, and now the dangerous gutter rip, a savagely moving narrow current rushing out beyond the dark blue water and onward toward the black threat of the reef, clutched at her.

Beatrice was borne along, foundering and twisting, the empty board swaying dangerously near her. Again she screamed as it swung closer to her, and then a new wave crashed over her, and for a moment she disappeared.

"She must have cramps, she's only moving her arms!" Audrey cried to Kamaki, who was on his board beside her. "I'm going to get her."

"No, let me do it, it's too dangerous, Aukele!"

But Audrey had dived off her board and was swimming out with fast, clean strokes toward the bobbing yellow cap. The wind was stronger now than ever, and the waves had become choppy and menacing. Another despairing cry rose from Beatrice, and again she disappeared below the dark blue water. But Audrey had reached her now and dived down to find her. Kamaki Marshall, grinding his teeth, furiously stroked forward, heedless of the current, his only wish that of saving Audrey, encumbered as she might be by the girl she was trying to save.

Now Audrey's head reappeared, and she was swimming slowly back on her side, an arm around Beatrice's chest. Kamaki Marshall reached her, and the two of them, swimming on each side of the half-conscious redhead, managed at last to reach the shore. The sky was darkening now, and out where the reef lurked, the water was as black as ink.

They knelt beside Beatrice, applying artificial respiration, forcing the water out of her lungs. Her right leg was drawn up at the knee, and there was an ugly, darkening bruise on her shin, where the loose surfboard had crashed against her after she had been tumbled into the water and drawn out by the gutter rip.

She groaned and slowly opened her eyes, her teeth chattering with pain. Audrey leaned toward her and soothingly murmured, "It's all right, Bea. You're safe. It's all over."

Beatrice Mason slowly raised her head, her face twisted with the pain of her injured shin. She saw the waves beyond, rising higher than ever, breaking off and crashing around the point. She closed her eyes for a moment, and then in a hoarse voice she gasped, "You saved me . . . and I tried to kill you."

"She's feverish with the pain, Kamaki. Look at her leg. That board must have hit her in the backwash."

"No . . . no . . . it's true. I did try to kill you, Audrey. There on the Pali, I was going to push you over, but Kamaki called you. And just now, with my surfboard. And you saved me, Audrey, in spite of what I did."

"But why should you want to kill me, Beatrice? Did you hate me so?" Tears stung Audrey's eyes as she stared at the pain-twisted face of her cousin.

"Yes. Because you were alive and Grover was dead. Because Daddy would have been ruined unless he could get your property. Fred Perry robbed him and ran away to Mexico. And then this man he met in Honolulu last year—oh, my leg hurts so, it hurts so!"

"Don't talk any more, Bea dear. We'll get you to a hospital."

"No." Beatrice shook her head. "I've got to tell you first. I've got to tell you everything. Daddy had a chance to sell your property for lots of money. He wasn't going to cheat you, just keep enough to get things back to where he wanted them to be. But I wanted to kill you because you had everything and I had nothing. And— and I wanted Kamaki, too."

Kamaki Marshall shook his head, his face grave with concern. "I couldn't ever have loved you, so all your scheming was for nothing. You have no love for this island nor for the brotherhood of man that exists here. In my classes I teach the children that their skin and

183

their creed mean nothing so long as they have kindness in their hearts to all who dwell upon this earth. I wish you had known that lesson, Beatrice. You wouldn't have known envy then or the greed that made you hate Aukele."

"I know it now." Beatrice Mason had closed her eyes and lay back, shuddering with the waves of agony from her injured leg. "Before we went on that drive around the island, I phoned that man Daddy had met. I told him where to find the conch shell—yes, I was there hiding in the garden when you and Kamaki were talking this morning. He was to dig up the shell and put another piece of paper into it. It was forged, and it showed that Daddy had bought the land from your father, Audrey. And then when I saw you and Kamaki standing there and looking at each other, I hated you, and I wanted you to die. And now you've every right to send me to prison where I belong."

Tears ran down Audrey's face as she shook her head and gently stroked the wet cheek of her cousin. "But I don't hate you, Beatrice. I'm sorry for you and for Uncle Dan. I told him I wanted to give him the land to pay him back. If he had come to me and told me how desperately he needed the money, I would have helped him. I was grateful to him. I like you, too, Beatrice, even though you never had much use for me. No, I won't be the one who sends you to prison. But now we're going to get you to a hospital and take care of that leg. Help me with her, Kamaki, please."

Chapter
TWENTY

BEATRICE MASON was propped up in a bed in the Queen's Hospital in the Punchbowl, not far from the War Memorial Cemetery, where the heroic Hawaiian soldiers of World War II were buried and where world-famous war correspondent Ernie Pyle lay at rest. Audrey and Kamaki Marshall had driven her first to the emergency clinic at Waimanalo, where her leg had been set; and then they had taken her to the hospital where she could rest and recuperate from the pain and shock.

It was the day after the surfing at Makapuu Point. Beatrice Mason had just finished telling her story to a detective of the Honolulu police force. The detective left the room to secure a warrant for the arrest of Estaban Aguinaldo and the latter's accomplice, who had been a clerk in the Bureau of Conveyances for the past decade. The clerk, having had ready access to the ledgers of tract title, had cleverly inserted the notation of the spurious quitclaim deed by which Dan Mason would have stood to take over the house and land on Waimanalo Beach. A third man, who had forged this quitclaim deed, would be arrested also.

Beatrice, humbly contrite, all her arrogance purged by her narrow escape from death and by the remorse of learning that it had been her intended victim who had saved her, had wanted to confess her own crime of attempted murder. But Audrey had steadfastly refused to allow her cousin to implicate herself. The original deed that made Audrey the true heiress to that coveted property was to be found, Beatrice had wanly told the detective, in an envelope addressed to her by Estaban Aguinaldo and left at the desk of the Royal Hawaiian.

She looked at Audrey and then at Kamaki Marshall, her eyes red and swollen, and stammered, "Daddy will go to prison too, won't he? He paid that man—he sold his prize jade chess set so he could have money to get Aguinaldo to have the deed forged and the clerk make that entry in the records. I wish you had let me drown out there yesterday. I'm so ashamed, and now I've ruined my father, too."

"I don't think so, Beatrice." Audrey's voice was compassionate. "Kamaki and I have talked to the detective. A bribe isn't altogether a criminal act in itself. Aguinaldo didn't have to take it, and he didn't have to forge the deed and have the clerk change the records. Their acts were criminal, yes. But I'm the only person that's really affected by all this, and I don't intend to bring charges against your father or against you, either."

Beatrice turned her face to one side and burst into helpless tears. Audrey looked at Kamaki and nodded, and they quickly left the room.

As she got into the Chevy, Audrey wiped her eyes with the handkerchief Kamaki Marshall had lent her. "It's been like a nightmare, Kamaki. Poor Bea—do you think they'll really let Uncle Dan go?"

"I don't know, Aukele. Of course, if you aren't going to prosecute, it might be difficult to convict him. But that realtor is certainly going to lose his license, the forger will go to jail, and the clerk most probably along with him. We'll dig up the conch shell together and tear up the forged deed. And then in October, there'll be nothing to stop your coming into your inheritance as your father and mother intended."

"How she must have hated me, just as she said, Kamaki—she had nothing and I had everything. She had even brought along a prescription for sleeping pills, and she would have dosed my coffee with them so that

186

she and that realtor could have time to switch the papers in the conch shell. She even said that she had thought of putting so many in my coffee that I would never awaken."

"You remember how I told you how one hunts the tiger?"

"Yes. I think I understand your allegory now. I was the decoy, wasn't I?"

He nodded, his eyes on the gleaming paved road ahead. It was the road that led to the top of the Pali. "Yes, you were, Aukele. You see, my father was the *haole* teacher whom your grandfather Kalaiki engaged to teach his daughter Milliama before she entered school."

"So that's how you knew who I was when I told you my name back in San Francisco?"

"Yes, Aukele. And when your mother grew up and married your father, Kalaiki told my father how much Philip Mason loved this beautiful island. And how his greatest joy was in the land your grandfather had sold him, so that he buried the deed to that land in the conch shell beneath the papaya tree. It was his way of showing that he loved and wanted to protect his dear ones for always. You couldn't have remembered me in those years when you played on the beach with your mother, Aukele, but I saw you many times. And then as I grew up, Luka became my very dear friend, and she told me how you had been taken from the island that was your home to live with others on the mainland who could not love you so much as Philip and Milliama and Luka herself did."

"But Kamaki, there's one thing that's been troubling me, more than it should, perhaps."

"And what's that, Aukele?"

She flushed and looked down, suddenly embarrassed at having given this one trivial thing so much weight. "You remember, back on the *Lurline*, when you said you weren't the one who'd walked past the house that night. And yet when I first saw you with Luka in my father's house, you admitted that you had been."

187

"I know." He gave her a sudden smile that was almost roguish. "That was a little white lie, and I ask your pardon for it, Aukele. You see, if I had told you aboard ship that I'd been the one, you would have started asking questions and shown me a lot of attention. Once I found out that your cousin was on board too, I wanted to meet her and learn what she was like. Somehow I think dear Luka must have had some kind of premonition about her, just from reading your letters, and even though you never said an unkind thing about her. Am I forgiven my lie?"

"Of course, Kamaki. Then you really did want to find me in San Francisco?"

"Yes. You see, Luka had told me how she had made you promise to keep the secret of the conch shell. But she didn't know that I already knew what that secret was, and because it was your secret, I would not reveal to her that I knew it. Then when she learned I was going to San Francisco during my time away from school, she asked me to try to find you and to tell you that you had a friend who would stand by you when it was time for you to come back home."

They had reached the summit of the Pali now. The car was parked in the same place where it had been early yesterday afternoon . . . an eternity ago, Audrey Mason thought as she walked with him to the rail and stared out toward the ocean.

"Yes, I've come home," she musingly repeated, "and I don't think I ever want to leave again, Kamaki. You know, back in San Francisco, I'd just finished my junior year at the university. I think I'd like to transfer my credits and take my degree here in Hawaii if I can."

"I'm sure that can be arranged, Aukele. And then what will you do?"

"My father was a schoolteacher, Kamaki. He knew what *aloha* truly meant, and so do you. Perhaps if I teach children too, I can remember it all my life."

He turned to look at her, and his face was no longer grave but smiling. And his blue eyes actually seemed to twinkle as he replied, "It seems I learned a good many of your secrets before you knew who I was, Aukele. I hope that you will stay here in Oahu and never leave again. Because in time, there will be secrets of mine which I hope you will come to know."

Audrey Mason blushed. She did not answer, but as they turned away from the rail and walked back to the car, their hands met and their fingers intertwined. And there was security and yet gentleness in his touch that made her think that she would not be a schoolteacher all her life—or that if she was, one day, when all this had been forgotten and she was free to set her own course, there might be children of her own to teach.

Rich in this new awareness, which because it was so new could take time to be savored, she could feel deep compassion for Beatrice, who would go back to live with her father in that gloomy house on Lombard Street, the two of them to live with such bitter memories. And she could think, with an even stronger compassion that was akin to genuine pity, of the final irony that even Beatrice had not understood—perhaps might never understand.

For she was remembering now what Beatrice had said to her as they unpacked in their room in the Royal Hawaiian, when the redhead had boasted that she had made a conquest of Kamaki Marshall. "He's a real man, not one of those half-breeds like the kind we saw diving for quarters and dimes at the dock." Yet as surely as she herself had the blood of two races in her veins, so did Kamaki. That was yet another bond between them. It was the strongest bond of all, because it was the bond that had made Hawaii the indomitable stronghold of the brotherhood of man.